THE SCALES
OF
ANUBIS

TRISH GAUNTLETT

 FriesenPress

One Printers Way
Altona, MB R0G 0B0
Canada

www.friesenpress.com

ISBN
978-1-03-830510-7 (Hardcover)
978-1-03-830509-1 (Paperback)
978-1-03-830511-4 (eBook)

Fiction, Mystery & Detective, Cozy, Books, Bookstores & Libraries

Distributed to the trade by The Ingram Book Company

Author's Note

This novel is a work of fiction. All characters (except those in the public domain) are purely fictitious. Any resemblance to actual persons, living or dead, is entirely coincidental. The village of Cascade Canyon, while fictional, is inspired by several close-knit villages on the North Shore of Vancouver, British Columbia. Many of the other places described, including the lost Japanese community hidden in the North Vancouver forest, are real.

For my mountaineer

On Howard Carter's gravestone

'May your spirit live, may you spend millions of years, you who love Thebes, sitting with your face to the north wind, your eyes beholding happiness. O night, spread thy wings over me as the imperishable stars.'

Inscribed on the Wishing Cup of King Tutankhamun

PROLOGUE

They would never find her. He was sure of that. He had hidden her where no one would ever look for someone supposed to be alive and travelling west. She was deep beneath the ground outside the fence of the old country churchyard now, separated from the consecrated dead. He smiled at the irony. She'd spent her life mocking the gods, ancient and modern. Now came the reckoning. Soon she'd face the Scales of Anubis. He knew her heart weighed more than the feather of Maat. It was made of stone. Her soul would not be granted immortality. She would be given to Ammit, the crocodile goddess, to devour and destroy. He didn't care. She was gone. She would never hurt them again. He finished the letters—his confession—and sealed them away. She'd be amused if she'd known their hiding place and that angered him, doing something to amuse her. He looked around the room as darkness fell. Candlelight flickered on the ancient artifacts, making their shadows dance. He knew Anubis would judge him too, for taking a life.

CHAPTER ONE

"Scott, can you help me with this box?"

Keeley Carisbrooke struggled to lift the heavy box from the floor outside the front door and gave up. She hoped it wasn't a pile of useless junk. Sometimes people donated things to second-hand shops instead of making the trip to the recycling bin where their worn-out ephemera belonged. Keeley and her staff at Past Life Emporium were schooled in opening boxes with gloves on, peering in gingerly, braced for what they might find.

"Where do you want it?" Scott scooped the box up with no trouble at all, glancing quickly in the direction of Sherine, hoping she'd noticed how strong and coordinated he was since he'd started Taekwondo.

Keeley smiled. She loved having the students at the shop. Her daughter Arwen (who had managed to live down her mother's obsession with *The Lord of the Rings*) had made friends with Scott Richards and Sherine Sasani in their first year at university and suggested that they all work Saturdays at Past Life to help with school expenses. Great idea for everyone. It meant that Keeley could keep the shop open six days a week.

Their fellow students came to visit them at the shop in search of the very affordable things Past Life offered, from clothes to books, kitchenware to CDs and DVDs (if they couldn't find machines Past Life sold those too) and furniture. And for other customers, those whose guilty secret was rummaging round thrift shops, consignment shops and second-hand shops, there were plenty of knick-knacks, collectibles and treasures to be found.

Keeley's choice of charities was another draw. She split a generous percentage of her profits between the library at the little local elementary school and the women's shelter, for reasons she shared only with her closest friends.

Scott took the box through to Keeley's cluttered desk in the storage room and headed back to the sales floor, where Sherine was helping a customer look through the china cabinets in search of Royal Albert's Greenwood Tree pattern. Although they always had a vague idea of what was in the shop they didn't keep a detailed inventory as things came and went so fast. Keeley tried to keep an eye on things coming in for some of the regulars with specific collections. She couldn't recall any Greenwood Tree but hoped Sherine and the customer would find a treasure.

Keeley wandered across the sales floor, browsing fondly through the showcases and shelves, straightening an old rug under the mid-century maple and oak furniture, and brushing some dust off a faux Tiffany lamp.

Past Life occupied the vast ground floor of an old ski lodge, its great cedar logs keeping it warm in winter and cool in summer, perfect for conserving second-hand things. It was divided in half, with sales in the huge room at the front and through a door, a storage and sorting room in the back. Keeley's desk was in the far corner of the storage room, surrounded by bins, boxes and shelves.

The storage room was brightly lit and warm. Keeley was glad of the warmth. There was a hint of frost in the air and the autumn leaves were turning red and gold across the forests surrounding Cascade Canyon, their village. They called it a village even though it was only ten minutes away from the bustling town centres on Vancouver's North Shore. It nestled on the side of Grouse Mountain, separated from the urban density by deep woods, in a world of its own. It had been one of the first places settled by travellers after first contact with British Columbia's First Nations. A hundred and fifty years ago, settlers built their cabins out of cedar and pine and made a living in forestry and fishing, huddling together against the harsh winters. Cascade Canyon had begun then, named for the mighty waterfall that plunged down the mountain and turned into a raging river running to the Pacific Ocean. Keeley's ancestors had come to Cascade Canyon in those days, making the dangerous journey from the Scottish Highlands to Canada's west. The sea was two days' ride on a strong horse then. Today it was twenty minutes away by car.

At the turn of the twentieth century people began to look up at the snowcapped mountains above their cabins and attempt to climb them. Soon they would ski on them, felling the biggest trees to clear the high ski runs. The lodge where Past Life made its home was built then, from those huge timbers. There were still faded initials carved in the rafters and rusty hooks for skis and sleds. Scott had discovered an old pair of snowshoes in a broken-down shed in the woods behind the shop. They were now proudly displayed over the front door, a reminder of the vibrant and mysterious past life of all second-hand things.

Keeley went back to her desk and examined the box. It was old, the cardboard darkened and stained, corners worn and torn. On the lid was a New York shipping label filled in with pen and ink, faded and illegible. There was an empty metal card holder on the side. She thought it looked like something from an archive. A collector would love this box, she thought. She carefully pulled open the old packing tape and looked inside. On the top were several magazines in blue paperback, all about archaeology. She put them in a pile on her desk. Underneath them were books. She reached for the one on top. It was wrapped in fabric, linen perhaps, she thought, once a bright colour but now faded to grey. She unwrapped it carefully and felt a little pulse of excitement as the book was revealed. The cover was the colour of desert sand. On the front, framed against a black square, was a gold scarab in the style of ancient Egypt. Embossed in gold, the title was a proclamation of discovery—*The Tomb of Tut Ankh Amen, Volume One by Howard Carter and A.C. Mace.*

Keeley didn't hesitate. She picked up the phone. "Loki? Can you come down? Can you come now?"

Loki Andresson owned Forest Folios, a rare book-shop on the top floor of the lodge, above Past Life. He was an avid outdoorsman, climber of high mountains. After climbing Mount Logan, Canada's highest peak, he'd challenged the big volcanoes in the Pacific Northwest—Rainier, Baker, St. Helen's, Hood, Shasta. Then he'd set his sights on Alaska's Denali. It was to be the first of his Seven Summits, the highest mountains on each of Earth's continents. He'd done all this when he was in his early twenties, nearly thirty years ago, building his experience into a successful mountain guiding company with clients from around the world. Then six years ago he'd followed his heart and mind, settled in Cascade Canyon and opened Forest Folios. People who'd known him in his mountaineering years were often surprised to find that his interests ran to the scholarly and arcane, evoking images of days spent in armchairs or at study desks rather than scaling the highest peaks. But he still went adventuring, climbing and exploring, sometimes closing Folios for days on end. It didn't matter to Loki. Much of his business was online and even when it wasn't, rare book collectors trusted him and were prepared to wait for his return.

Loki always entered a room at speed. He was tall, with a mountaineer's lean build and vital energy. He came striding into the storage room through the lodge's back door and covered the ground to Keeley's desk in record time. She smiled up at him with affection. They had not yet fully explored their feelings for each other but she knew they both felt the same delightful tension when they were together. For now, they were happy to be close friends. Keeley hoped it would become something more, but life had taught her caution and patience.

Loki didn't even look at her. He'd caught sight of the book. She understood. It was his passion. It gave him the same sense of excitement as a new trail or an untracked snowfield. He took a deep breath and reached for it, and suddenly remembering she was there, raised his eyebrows to ask her permission. She nodded, still smiling, and he picked it up reverently.

"Where did you get this?" he asked.

"It was in this box that someone left outside the front door last night," she answered, reaching down to show him the box. "There was no note or name on it but that's not unusual. I thought the books might be old as soon as I opened the box but then I saw this one and I knew I had to call you right away."

Loki opened it and they looked at the first page with its strange designs.

"Tutankhamun, ruler of Upper Heliopolis," Loki said quietly. "Throne name Nebkheperura."

"You can read that?" Keeley asked, amazed. "Is it hieroglyphics?"

Loki laughed. "No, of course I can't, but every book-seller knows this book. We all dream of finding it. Those ovals are called cartouches. They hold the symbols of important names. I've always been drawn to books about Egyptian archaeology and I've read this book—one of the later printings though—not the first edition."

"Do you think that's what this is, a first edition?" she asked as he turned the page again. "Is it genuine?"

"I think so," said Loki. "Look at this. '*Cassell and Company, Ltd. London, New York, Toronto and Melbourne 1923.*' Howard Carter found the tomb in 1922 and published this a year later with photos by Harry Burton. Burton took thousands of images of the excavation and the tomb."

Loki turned the page again. A card had been slipped inside. On the card, a signature—*Howard Carter, 1924.* They both looked at it in awe.

"This is an amazing find, Keeley," said Loki. "Signed by Carter himself!"

Keeley gazed at the name, fascinated. "I've heard of him, of course, but I don't know much about him," she said.

"He started as an archaeologist when he was just a seventeen-year old English boy looking for adventure in Egypt," said Loki. "He was a wonderful artist and he was hired to make drawings at the Temple of Queen Hatshepsut, in Thebes. But it wasn't until he met the Earl of Carnarvon and found the treasures of Tutankhamun's tomb in the Valley of the Kings that the whole world knew his name."

Keeley was surprised. "I didn't know you were interested in ancient Egypt," she said, smiling up at him.

"I'm just a man of mystery," he said with a grin.

They looked at each other for a long moment and Keeley thought about the intriguing implications of that statement. Then she looked back at the book. "You should take it, Loki," she said. "Take it up to Folios where it can be properly researched and conserved."

Loki put the autographed card back in the book and closed it carefully. "Keeley, this book might be valuable," he said. "The signature too. If they're genuine they're worth hundreds, perhaps thousands of dollars. I'll take the book and authenticate it but I wonder if we should try to find whoever dropped it off here. They obviously didn't know what they had."

"Yes, of course," said Keeley. "This has happened to us before. People have left things with real or sentimental value in donated items. I'll get in touch with the Cascade Courier and ask them to put a notice in the paper for us. But let's see if it's real first."

Loki nodded and turned away, lost in thought.

"Oh wait," said Keeley, "I almost forgot. It was wrapped in this."

She handed him the faded piece of linen. He gazed at it in wonder.

"Keeley, I think this is very old, ancient, in fact," said Loki, "I've seen some things like this in displays of Egyptian grave goods."

"You should take it with the book," said Keeley, "but let's show it to Scott first."

She called the students in to tell them about the discovery. Scott, who was in Ancient Mediterranean and Near Eastern studies at the University of British Columbia, was over the moon. "Can I take photos?" he asked Keeley. "This is going on all my social media platforms. It'll be all over the net once the Egyptomaniacs pick it up. Amazing!"

"Of course," she laughed. They all loved Scott's enthusiasm for ancient Egypt.

Scott asked Loki to hold the book, open the cover and then hold up the linen cloth, while he took photos from all angles.

"Thanks Loki," he said. "Wow! I can't believe it. Keeley, is it OK if I sit back here and post it right now? It's not busy out front."

She nodded. "Can you take pictures of the box, too, Scott? Then if someone brought it here by mistake they'll get in touch." Scott did as she asked, then sat down in a chair in the corner and devoted himself to his phone, tapping away. Arwen and Sherine went back into the store, chatting excitedly about the book.

Loki put the cloth back on Keeley's desk. "This should be looked at by an expert. We could see if Elizabeth can recommend someone."

Elizabeth Liang was a costume designer, in constant demand from Vancouver's thriving movie industry. She was a regular at Past Life, digging through piles of fabric and bric-a-brac for material she could remake into something spectacular.

"I'll call her today," said Keeley. "Until then, could you take it up to Folios with the book please? I think it's safer in your temperature-controlled environment. I don't want it just sitting here on my desk until we open on Monday."

"Sure," said Loki as he headed for the door. He stopped in the doorway and looked back at her.

"This feels like the beginning of an adventure, doesn't it?" he said. "A mystery, complete with Egyptian artifacts and hints of an ancient tomb."

As he spoke, the wind, cold and invasive, found its way in and swept across the floor towards Keeley. She shivered and her imagination conjured an echo, a whisper, a sigh, across three thousand years.

"Close the door, Loki," she said. "The cold is getting in."

CHAPTER TWO

On Monday morning Keeley walked into Bean Cabin coffee shop next door to Past Life to find Elizabeth Liang just settling in at a cozy table. Bean Cabin was always bustling and Keeley knew almost everyone in there. She navigated around the piles of garment bags Elizabeth always carried with her and sat down across from the costume designer. They both waved to Yvonne, behind the counter. Yvonne and Keeley had been friends since Grade Four. Yvonne was the only person in the world allowed to call her Kee.

"Hi Kee, hi Elizabeth!" Yvonne called out. "Usual?"

The both nodded and turned back to each other and the business at hand.

"This sounds exciting," said Elizabeth, leaning forward to make herself heard above the chatter of conversation. "Tell me everything!"

Keeley leaned forward too but kept her voice low. All her instincts were telling her to be discreet about what they'd found. She didn't know where it was coming from, but a small ripple of apprehension was beginning to creep in. She hesitated.

"What is it?" Elizabeth sensed her hesitation and peered at her anxiously. "What's wrong?"

Superstition, Keeley thought, just superstition. She smiled at Elizabeth. "Nothing, nothing at all. I'm being silly. It's just so mysterious and I feel so responsible for its safety for some reason. But you're right, it is exciting."

Peter, Yvonne's husband, brought their order to the table—two huge mugs of dark roasted coffee and two cream horns. They beamed up at him. He was a big, bluff, friendly man who'd been a logger in British Columbia's remote forests, but after marrying Yvonne he'd decided that his real calling was pastry chef. They'd owned Bean Cabin for fifteen years and were among the happiest people Keeley knew. It was impossible to come to Bean Cabin without having one of Peter's pastries.

"There's more where those came from," said Peter proudly, before heading back to the kitchen.

Keeley put milk in her coffee and stirred it distractedly. "I told you most of it on the phone, I think," she said to Elizabeth, "about the book and the wrapping. I think it's linen and Loki thinks it's old. We need an expert who can authenticate it. It will go a long way towards creating a provenance for the book."

"I'd love to see it," said Elizabeth. "I'll know whether or not it's linen but I won't be able to tell its age. Being in the movie industry all these years has taught me that you can replicate a certain age in anything, even people!"

She laughed and her face lit up with the smile her friends loved so much. Elizabeth was striking— beautiful enough to be a movie star—but she'd always wanted to be on the designing side of film production. At thirty-four she was one of the industry's foremost costume designers. She split her time between Los Angeles and Vancouver. Keeley had wondered once if she'd ever be lured away permanently to the big cities south of the border, but Vancouver's 'Hollywood North' had sustained a flourishing movie industry for decades and was still one of North America's top shooting locations.

"Let's go up to Loki's when we finish here," said Keeley.

They sampled Peter's cream horns with delight and Elizabeth gave a big thumbs up to Peter, who'd kept glancing through the kitchen doorway to see their reaction. Satisfied, he went back to his flaky pastry.

"I do know someone who might be able to help with the fabric," Elizabeth said, as they sipped their coffee. "We used him as a consultant on one of the movies I costumed. His name is Charles Deeds and he's an expert in ancient textiles and Egyptian artifacts, which is an interesting coincidence. He studied at Cambridge and is on the faculty of the Institute of Archaeology at University College London, but he travels around a lot to consult. We try to have tea together whenever we're in the same place. He's a nice guy with old-school manners, very private and quite reserved. I can get in touch with him, if you like."

"That would be great," said Keeley.

They finished their coffee, regretfully declined another of Peter's pastries and went next door to Past Life.

Declan and Rory were there. Declan was helping a customer look through some old records and Rory was behind the counter. Rory and Declan had moved to

Cascade Canyon five years ago after selling their big-city law practice and retiring. They were completely different in personality but for them it was a case of opposites attracting. They'd been work and life partners for thirty-five years. Keeley was so grateful to have them at Past Life. They were there every weekday, coming in early and staying late—for the love of doing it. They both gave pro bono legal advice to those who needed it at the women's shelter, although Keeley could never see where they found the time. A quiet retirement wasn't for them. They filled their lives by volunteering on non-profit boards, travelling whenever they could find something they thought was affordable (they were very well-off, but thrifty—Rory always joked that it was his Scottish ancestry) and generous to a fault. Keeley wished she could pay them more but her business model was heavily skewed towards raising charitable funds. She guessed that they donated most of their wages to the women's shelter anyway.

"Hi you two!" Rory called out. "How were Peter's pastries?" He smiled broadly under an unruly thatch of red-grey hair and turned the intensity of his startling blue eyes on both of them. In his mid-sixties Rory was as strong and vital as a much younger man and was still on the receiving end of many appreciative glances. He was outgoing and social, perfect for the front desk of a busy store. He and Elizabeth launched into a lively discussion about the movie she was currently working on. Rory wondered whether it would be better than the book and Elizabeth promised to go and see it with him as soon as it was released.

Keeley tuned in to the conversation Declan was having. In complete contrast to Rory, Declan's hair was smooth and dark, with a single streak of grey falling over his emerald green eyes. He was talking quietly and seriously to the customer, who had narrowed down her search to three Deutsche Grammophon albums from the '60s and '70s, all of them Beethoven, played by the Berlin Philharmonic under Herbert von Karajan. Declan's profound love of classical music had led him to a level of expertise rarely found outside the music profession. His interests were wide-ranging, from Bach to contemporary classical. He had built the store's record collection to a point where it drew collectors from all over Vancouver's Lower Mainland, sometimes even from Washington and Oregon. He used all this knowledge now, to help his customer with her selection. Happily, she decided to take all three and Declan came with her to the counter to make the purchase. Rory took over and Declan turned to Keeley and Elizabeth.

"Good morning to you both," he said. There were still traces of Dublin in his accent. His friends teased him about it but they loved to hear him speak. He was a poet, a music lover, a dreamer, and had been a fierce and formidable opponent in the court room—his calm, composed voice belying the steel it wielded. His loyalty to his friends, once they had earned his trust, was indestructible.

Elizabeth gave him a hug. "Declan, I haven't seen you for ages! How are you? What are you up to?"

"Nothing at all, dear one," he said, with a quick smile. "Just working here at Past Life, the occasional concert or two and of course, doing all the work at home so this one..." he tossed his head at Rory "…can keep up with his films and fancy meals."

Rory laughed and reached across the counter to whack Declan on the shoulder. "Sure an' 'tis a sad t'ing y'are, mo chroí," he said in a dreadful attempt at an Irish accent.

Declan sighed. "You see what I have to endure." Even the customer was smiling now and Keeley thought what a happy and harmonious bunch they were, doing work they loved in good company.

The bell on the front door chimed as the customer closed it behind her.

"What's this about a book, now?" said Rory immediately. "I ran into Loki on my way in and he told me about it."

"I don't know any more than I did yesterday," said Keeley, "but Elizabeth's going to come up to Loki's with me now to look at the fabric it was wrapped in. She knows someone who might help us date it."

"Keep us posted!" said Rory.

"Of course," said Keeley.

They went through to the back room. Keeley noticed the pile of archaeology magazines on her desk. She'd glanced through the other books and finding nothing else that stood out, had put them back in the box to sort through later. She pushed the box under her desk and made a mental note to get Loki to have a look at them as well.

Loki threw the door open as they walked up the back steps to Forest Folios. It was a small shop, only half the size of Past Life, filled with bookshelves and glass cases, with the air of a library in an old country estate. Two deep and worn green leather chairs were placed by the window, each with a small side table and a reading lamp. Loki never rushed his customers. They could sit and look at books for as long as they wanted.

In the back corner, next to the door leading to the little kitchen, Loki kept a small standing desk that doubled as a counter. A multi-lens magnifier with its own light was attached to the side. Carter's book was there, resting on its linen wrapping. Loki was taking advantage of a lull between customers to examine it.

"Elizabeth, come and see," he said, with an excited look at Keeley as they walked towards the back.

"Can I touch it? Do I need gloves?" Elizabeth asked. Keeley had been wondering about gloves as well, feeling guilty about handling the book without them the night before.

"Most people think that, but you don't," said Loki. "In fact, we warn against it. Just clean, dry, bare hands. No hand lotion?" he asked.

"No," said Elizabeth. "I don't like to use it while I'm handling fabrics."

She picked up the book and turned it over, gently. "OK to open it?" she asked.

Loki nodded. "I've taken the autographed card out and put it in a protective sleeve so it's fine."

She opened the front cover. Opposite the title page there was a photograph of the Earl of Carnarvon.

"Carnarvon sponsored the excavation," Loki said. "Carter had spent six years in the Valley of the Kings without much to show for his efforts but then in November of 1922 he found a series of steps cut into the valley floor, leading to a sealed doorway. He knew he'd discovered something important and he cabled Carnarvon in England to come to Egypt immediately. As soon as Carnarvon arrived they went down the steps together and Carter made a small hole in the sealed doorway, held up a candle to the hole and peered through."

"Wonderful things," said Elizabeth, softly.

Keeley looked at her in surprise.

"I worked on a documentary about this once," Elizabeth said. "Carter was asked if he could see anything and he said, 'Yes, wonderful things.'"

Keeley had seen the photos of the treasure—dazzling gold objects, jewels, wooden animals, painted furniture and chariots, golden goddesses and the massive blue and gold mask of Tutankhamun himself.

The three friends stood in silence for a long time, gazing at the book that Carter had touched, transported to the Egyptian desert a century ago, when a sleeping pharoah had woken to captivate the world.

Loki broke their reverie. "Five months later Carnarvon was dead. The curse of Tutankhamun entered our imaginations then and has stayed there, although there's no evidence, just superstition."

Keeley felt the same whispering brush of fear that had touched her the night before. Here in Loki's old-world bookshop anything seemed possible. She wanted to warn them, tell them not to touch the book, to hide it away where no one would find it.

She pulled herself together, annoyed by these otherworldly thoughts. She was a pragmatic and practical person. Where was all this coming from?

"What about the fabric, Elizabeth?" she asked. "What do you think?"

Elizabeth put the book down and picked up the faded fabric. "Definitely linen," she said. "Old, I think, very old, but I can't be sure. Loki, can you keep it here until I can get Charles Deeds to have a look at it?"

"Who?" said Loki. "Sounds like a character out of one of my books."

"You'll think that when you meet him, too," said Elizabeth, smiling. "Sherlock Holmes, or perhaps Howard Carter himself. Charles is a quiet and studious man. I don't know much about his private life but he has an international reputation as an authority on ancient Egypt. I've worked with him before and consider him a friend, although we don't see each other often because he's living in England. Keeley and I have talked about it and I'm going to contact him."

"Good," said Loki. He wrapped the book in the linen cloth and went to a small safe built into the wall, well hidden by his desk. "The safe is humidity and temperature controlled," he said. "They'll be fine in there until the expert can have a look at them."

They chatted for a while and Elizabeth left, promising to update them about Charles Deeds.

"Well, I should get back downstairs," said Keeley. "See you later, Loki."

"Want to grab some pizza after work?" he asked.

"Sure," said Keeley. "How about a short hike first? We could go up the canyon from the fish hatchery to the dam. Earn the pizza."

"Sounds great! Meet you at six o'clock downstairs?" Keeley could hear Loki's love for the woods in his voice and she knew that they would enjoy the hike even more in each other's company.

"Done!" she said. "Let's hope the rain holds off. I can feel something in the air."

CHAPTER THREE

It was dusk when Keeley and Loki met outside Past Life, but the skies were still clear. They'd both brought head-lamps. Like lots of people who lived in Cascade Canyon they kept hiking gear at work to make the most of the spectacular surroundings.

The hike they were going on was easy but anything could happen, even to the most experienced hikers, so they wore proper clothes and boots, brought water and snacks and checked that their phones were fully charged. Loki carried bear spray. Bears were increasingly active in the area, busily trying to eat enough to get through winter. They were still wide awake so it was best to avoid encounters. Bear spray was a last resort, but a good idea.

It took nearly two hours to go up and down the trail. Keeley and Loki chatted happily, went to visit a giant old cedar tree just off the path and looked for mushrooms. Loki was an expert in mycology and loved to photograph them. Keeley wouldn't touch them unless he said it was OK. There were several poisonous kinds growing in the forests of British Columbia and every year they claimed lives. The worst was *Amanita phalloides* or death cap. It was invasive, having shown up in BC in the late 1990s. Because it was such a newcomer many people didn't recognize it and made the mistake of gathering it for food. Loki pointed one out to Keeley. She could see how easy it would be to mistake it for the benign, edible mushrooms many people foraged for in these woods.

At about eight o'clock they came down the path behind their shops and Keeley noticed a light on in Past Life.

"Declan must be working late," she said. "He sometimes comes back to sort through the music if we get a new donation of records or CDs."

"I'll just go up and drop off my gear, then we'll go for pizza," said Loki, starting up the steps to Folios as Keeley opened the back door to Past Life. Shock pulsed through her. "Loki! Loki!" she called, fear in her voice.

He rushed back downstairs and found her standing in the doorway. The storage room was a scene of devastation. Her desk had been ransacked, papers were scattered everywhere, the drawers were upturned and empty, cupboards were open, contents strewn around. There was broken glass and china on the floor. Keeley started to go inside but Loki stopped her.

"Wait Keeley," he said. "We're calling the police. We don't want to touch anything and we have to be sure whoever did this is gone."

That thought made her shudder and he put his arm around her, pulling her close to him. She was grateful and stayed there a moment, gaining her equilibrium. Fear was beginning to be replaced by anger. "Who would do this? Why would anyone do this?" she said.

Loki was on the phone with the police. "On their way," he told Keeley.

"This just has to be vandalism," Keeley said. "There's nothing of value here. We don't even have an alarm, never needed it. It's just second-hand stuff, nothing that…we never have…" she trailed off, looking up at him. They'd both had the same thought.

Loki nodded. "Carter's book. Could it really be that?"

"Isn't it only worth a few hundred dollars?" she said. "Not worth doing all of this. And hardly anyone knows we have it."

"Remember that Scott put it all over social media on Saturday," said Loki. "Instant world-wide information. If it's not the book, it's a very big coincidence." He leaned into the shop, trying to get a look at Keeley's desk. "What happened to the rest of the books in that box?"

She peered in. The box was missing. "They're gone," she said, in disbelief. "I put them back in the box so I could show you tomorrow. The box is gone."

Loki stepped back outside. "Keeley, I've got to check Folios. If they know about the book… Come with me. I don't want to leave you alone down here." He raced up the stairs with Keeley behind him but when he unlocked the door to Folios the alarm went off, the lights went on and they both saw with relief that nothing had been touched. Whoever had come to steal Carter's book hadn't guessed it was in Loki's safe. He opened the safe and checked to make sure, carefully locking it again.

They heard the sirens then and went downstairs just as the police arrived.

Corporal Luc Gagnon was part of the North Vancouver RCMP detachment. He'd lived in Cascade Canyon for five years and was a popular and respected member of the community. He often came to community gatherings with his family and sometimes hiked with Loki. Keeley thought of him as a friend.

"Keeley. Loki." He spoke sharply, with a quick glance at them. He was scanning around, checking the path, the woods, the back lane beside the shops. "I was on call tonight. Have you been inside?"

"No," said Keeley, "we didn't want to touch anything before you got here and we didn't know if he…if they were still here."

"Good," Luc said briskly. "The forensic team is on its way. I'm going in. You come behind me."

They picked their way through the debris. Shock was beginning to set in again for Keeley. She stumbled and Loki caught her arm. They made their way slowly to the connecting door between the storage room and the shop. Luc opened it. It was dark. Keeley thought that was a good sign. Whoever had broken in hadn't risked being seen from the street. She reached past Luc's shoulder, turned on the light and gasped in horror.

Declan lay at their feet, unmoving. Blood poured from a wound on his head.

"Declan," she whispered, dropping down to the floor beside him. The tears came now and she sobbed. "Oh no. Declan please."

Luc and Loki were beside her. Gently, Luc felt for a pulse. It seemed like an eternity until he pulled the radio from his belt and spoke into it. "Dispatch, send an ambulance to the Past Life store on Cedar Street in Cascade Canyon. We have an unconscious male, head injury. Make it fast—no time to lose here."

The quick wave of relief that Declan was still alive gave way to terror again. He was so pale, so still. Keeley reached for his hand and held it. So cold.

"Where is he? Declan! I knew something was wrong!" Rory came running into the store through the back door, oblivious to the wreckage in the storage room. He fell to the floor beside Declan and started to gather him into his arms. Luc restrained him. "Don't Rory. Don't. It's a head injury. Don't move him."

Rory crumpled onto the floor. Loki knelt beside him and put an arm round his shoulder. "It'll be OK buddy," he said. "He's strong and help is on its way. Just hang in there."

The paramedics arrived first, followed closely by the forensic team, who held back until Declan could be stabilized, put on a stretcher and carried to the ambulance. He was still unconscious. Rory was holding his hand.

"I'm going to follow them in my car," said Loki to Keeley. "I'll let you know as soon as there's any news."

"Keeley," said Luc Gagnon. "Let's walk through the store and you can tell me if anything's missing."

Keeley tried to concentrate. "Loki and I think we know what this is about, Luc," she said. "It's a long story. Let's go back to my desk. I need to make a quick call to Arwen and tell her I'm OK. She's at home and this news will be getting out soon."

There were anxious voices at the back door. "Keeley!" It was Yvonne.

"Can I…?" Keeley looked at Luc for direction.

"Of course," he said. "As quickly as you can, though."

She went to the back door and found Yvonne and Peter with Arwen, Scott and Sherine. Word travelled fast in the village. A uniformed officer was stopping them from coming in. Arwen threw her arms around her mother and held her tight.

"Oh Mum, I was so anxious when I heard all the sirens, then Scott phoned me and said it was Past Life so I came straight here. Are you OK? Is everyone OK?"

Keeley told them about Declan. She couldn't hold back the tears. Yvonne put her arms around her. They were all shocked into silence. Then Peter, strong and kind, said, "Let's go next door and make some coffee for Keeley and the police team. At least that's something we can do."

Arwen was reluctant to leave but Scott and Sherine linked their arms through hers and walked her away. Thank goodness for friendship, thought Keeley. It will get us all through this.

She went back to join Luc. He motioned to her to sit down at her desk, righted an overturned chair and joined her, getting out his notebook and pen.

"Tell me the long story," he said.

She started with finding the box on the front steps of the store and ended with checking to make sure the book was still in Loki's safe.

"The box is gone," she told Luc. "They must have taken it and the rest of the books that were in it." A thought occurred to her and she started to sort through the wreck-age on her desk. "There were some magazines in the box too," she explained to Luc. She found them under a pile of folders. "Still here. So it was the books they were after. Could this be about more than just Carter's book? Something else?"

"Maybe," said Luc, "but it looks as if the book was the target. They came in the back way, trashed the place until they found the box of books. Then they heard something in the store and ran into Declan. After Declan…" he paused and shook his head angrily at the thought of what had happened. "After attacking Declan they got out of here fast, grabbing the box of books on the way."

He frowned. "If all this is about the book," he said, "someone's willing to do anything to get their hands on it. I'm worried about you and the staff, Keeley. Worried about Loki too although whoever did this didn't think of check-ing Folios. How would you feel—I'll run this past Loki as well—if we publish a press release saying we think the book might have been the target of a violent robbery and we've taken it into police custody as evidence? We won't really do that. We can't protect it the way Loki's special safe can, but it will direct attention away from here."

She nodded. "Makes sense, Luc. I'm sure Loki will agree. Is there anything else I need to do?"

"Well, let's walk through the shop to make sure nothing else has been taken, but I'm convinced now that it must be about Carter's book. There's more to this."

They looked carefully through the storage room and the shop where the forensic team was taking samples, dusting for fingerprints. Luc told them to pay special attention to the area around Keeley's desk.

Keeley stopped suddenly at the place where Declan had been hurt. She looked down at the floor. There was a red stain on it and she couldn't bear it.

Luc noticed. "I'll get the team to clean that up after we have samples, Keeley. We can't help with the rest of this mess but at least we can do that."

She thanked him and turned away, wondering if she would ever walk by that spot again without seeing blood.

CHAPTER FOUR

Next morning Keeley, Scott, Sherine and Arwen gathered in the back room of the store. The students were all in their third year now with flexible schedules so they were taking time off from classes. Everyone was acutely aware that Rory and Declan weren't with them. Keeley put a 'Closed until further notice' sign on the front door and they all turned their attention to cleaning up the mess.

They had permission from Luc and the forensic team to put things back in order, with instructions to call him if anything else was missing. Nothing was. Yvonne and Peter sent over coffee and sandwiches and just as they all sat down to take a break Loki came in. He looked tired and drawn but he didn't keep them waiting.

"Declan's conscious," he said, "and he's going to be OK."

They all spoke at once. "Oh thank God!" "Wow! He's a tough guy!" "Rory must be so happy!" "When can we see him?"

Loki laughed and put his hands up in mock self-defense. "It's going to be a while before we can see him," he answered. "He just needs rest and quiet and they'll be observing him for a few days in hospital to make sure he's recovering well. Rory will let us know. By the way, Rory is worried about how you'll manage here. I told him to forget all that. We'll take care of things here. His job is to take care of Declan."

"Of course he's thinking about us first," said Keeley. "That's just Rory."

"I'll go up to Folios and put a closed sign on the door," said Loki. "My customers are used to me keeping odd hours. Then I'll come back here and help."

Keeley breathed out a long, slow breath. She was beginning to feel normal again. Declan would be OK and so would Rory. All the people she loved were safe and most of them were right here with her. She picked up her coffee cup and raised it in a toast.

"To Declan!" she said. "May he be back here with us soon."

"Declan!" they echoed, clinking their coffee mugs together in relief. Then they got back to work.

It took them two days, working from dawn to dusk, to put Past Life back in order. Keeley gave the archaeology magazines from the box to Loki for safekeeping. She couldn't bring herself to look at them yet. Yvonne and Peter kept them supplied with food, many people from the village stopped by to offer help and support, Keeley had an alarm system installed and there were no more incidents.

Elizabeth had called as soon as word of the break-in reached her. Keeley assured her that they were all OK, especially Declan.

Elizabeth was intrigued that the robbery seemed to centre around the book. "That makes it even more likely the linen is genuine," she said. "I have a call in to Charles Deeds. As soon as I hear back from him I'll let you know."

Luc Gagnon had put a police report in the Vancouver papers and posted it to online news sites.

> *A robbery at Past Life Emporium in Cascade Canyon on Monday was foiled by employee Declan Rellene, who was injured and is recovering in hospital. All indications point to the target of the robbery being a rare book, The Tomb of Tut Ankh Amen, Volume One by Howard Carter and A.C. Mace. Thanks to Mr. Rellene the book was not found by the thieves and is now in the custody of the North Vancouver RCMP. If you saw anything suspicious at or near Past Life on Monday night or have any information about this violent robbery attempt please contact Cpl. Luc Gagnon at the North Vancouver RCMP Detachment.*

On Thursday Keeley decided to reopen Past Life. Scott, Sherine and Arwen were still flexing their university schedules, so although Keeley missed Rory and Declan she had lots of help. As soon as word went out that Past Life was open again people from the village flooded in, some out of curiosity, most just to show support. They bought treasures and trinkets, chatted happily with the staff and poured positive energy back into the space.

On Friday Rory came in through the back door. He looked tired, thinner and happy.

They all gathered round him, hugging him, making him sit down, running for a cup of tea for him and peppering him with questions until he laughed and said, "Right, all of you! I'm going to tell it just once, so all of you sit down and listen.

"Declan has told Luc all of this—what he remembers anyway. He was in the front of the store picking out some records for a customer who had emailed him with a special request. Being Declan…" Rory's voice wavered but he shook it off and carried on. "Being Declan, he was absorbed in the music and stayed later than he realized. That's why I was coming to get him. We'd planned to go to the pub for dinner.

"He was just packing up the records when he heard someone crashing around here in the back. He thought it was one of us and that we'd fallen or dropped something, so he called out. He called my name actually…" Rory took a deep breath and went on. "Then he came running to help. As he opened the door he saw someone coming towards him, a man, stocky, in dark clothes. He didn't recognize him. The man charged him and…and that's all he remembers." Rory stopped and brushed his hands across his eyes.

They all moved to comfort him. Arwen got there first, kneeling in front of him, taking his hands in hers and saying gently, "It's OK Rory, it's all over. He's going to be fine and we'll all be here for both of you, anything you need, anytime."

Rory smiled down at Arwen. "Thank you, dear one," he said. "Thanks to all of you. We couldn't get through this without you. And as for me, I'm coming back to work!"

The murmurs of protest from the rest of them were unconvincing. They wanted him here where they could keep an eye on him.

"Right!" said Keeley briskly. "Back at it, all of you! Rory, could you have a look at the china and collectibles, all the things in the glass cases under the counter? I don't think anything's been touched but I'd like to be sure and you know that stuff better than any of us."

Rory stood up with determination. Arwen slipped her arm through his and they walked towards the open door connecting the back room with the front of the store. As they reached the door Rory looked down at the floor and stumbled a bit but Arwen held onto him tightly and moved him through. They started to look at the collectibles together and soon Keeley could hear them laughing. She smiled to herself, thinking that perhaps some magic had attached itself to her daughter when she'd named her for Tolkien's gentle elf princess.

Gradually life was returning to normal. Another week passed with Declan getting stronger every day. Two weeks after the attack he was released and sent home. Keeley closed the store for the day. She and the others decorated Rory's and Declan's place as if was New Year's Eve and were all waiting on the porch when Declan arrived home with Rory on one side of him and Loki on the other. If they were shocked by his frailty they didn't show it. They knew he would be back with them soon, in full strength, listening quietly to his music.

Declan's face lit up when he saw them all. "Ah, you dear things!" he said. "Just what I need now, your lovely faces."

They helped him inside, sat him in his favourite chair and got him tea and a whole plate of Peter's pastries. Arwen put a Gershwin record on. No sad music today. The whole house was filled with flowers. They asked him no questions.

After about half an hour, Keeley could see that he was getting tired. "OK everyone," she said, "let's get out of here and let Declan rest. He knows we'll be making pests of ourselves visiting him every day anyway."

She kissed him gently on his cheek, still dark with bruises. "Welcome home, dear friend," she whispered.

They all set off happily on their own errands. Keeley decided to go back to Past Life. There was still lots of paperwork to catch up on and she'd have the quiet time she needed to do it while the store was closed. She was working through the bank statements, allocating the monthly amounts to the women's shelter and the school library when her cell phone rang. It was Elizabeth.

"Hi Keeley, how are you? How's Declan?"

"He's home and doing well," said Keeley. "I know he'd love to see you."

"I'll come as soon as I can," she said. "But I have some news. I heard from Charles Deeds this morning. He's been travelling in the Middle East and didn't get his messages until he got home to London. When I told him about the linen and the book he insisted on knowing all about it, all the details. I even told him about the break-in and that we thought the book was the target. His response was quite guarded, even more so than usual and I thought perhaps he wasn't interested. Then he said suddenly that he didn't want to talk about it anymore on the phone. He said he'd get the next plane out of Heathrow and be in Vancouver tomorrow. I was surprised. But he was adamant."

Keeley felt a wave of apprehension. "That's so strange," she said. "His reaction seems to be really over the top. He knows something we don't, doesn't he?"

"That's the impression I got," said Elizabeth, "but he absolutely refused to discuss it further on the phone. I guess we'll just have to wait until tomorrow. I'm meeting him at the airport in the morning. Shall I bring him straight to Past Life?"

"Yes, bring him here. We can talk privately in the back room. And I think if he knows something that could shed light on the break-in and the attack on Declan I need to have Luc Gagnon here as well," said Keeley. "I'll ask him to join us. Loki too."

"Good idea," said Elizabeth. "We should be there around mid-day. See you then."

"Elizabeth wait," said Keeley, anxiously. "Is there any reason for us—you as well—to worry about our safety where Charles Deeds is concerned?"

"No, not at all," said Elizabeth. "I've known Charles for years. He's very private and reserved, but completely harmless. He's just being really mysterious about all this."

"OK, see you tomorrow then," Keeley said.

After talking to Elizabeth, Keeley tried to get back to the accounts. But the numbers swam in front of her eyes and she gave up. She walked through the closed store, straightening up the old sheet music in Declan's corner, her mind filling with questions for Charles Deeds, troubled by the danger that might lie in the answers.

CHAPTER FIVE

They waited in the back room. Keeley had gathered chairs around her desk and ordered coffee and pastries from Bean Cabin. Yvonne and Peter kept trying to refuse payment but Keeley insisted. It helped her feel that things were back to normal.

Rory was looking after the front of the store. Scott and Sherine were in class but Arwen had stopped by to help Rory. It was a quiet day and Rory could have easily managed alone but being together helped both Arwen and Rory feel safe and useful.

Loki was helping himself to a cream horn when Luc Gagnon arrived. He'd parked his police car a couple of blocks away and walked down the back lane. There'd been enough attention on Past Life recently. He didn't want to set tongues wagging again. He shook off the cold as he walked in.

"Coffee. Great! And are those Peter's cream horns?" Luc asked. It was a rhetorical question. He knew very well what they were and was already helping himself. "Any word from Elizabeth?"

"She messaged me about an hour ago to say they were leaving the airport," said Keeley. "They should be here any minute." She walked to the connecting door to the shop and closed it. She didn't want Rory to relive past events as they talked to Charles Deeds.

Luc filled them in on the investigation so far. No witnesses except Declan, no useful fingerprints, no way to trace who'd dropped off the box of books. "At some point," Luc said, "we'll put out a request to the general public for information about who dropped off the box. But I don't want to alert anyone yet. The box is the only lead we've got."

A lot was riding on Charles Deeds.

They didn't have long to wait. They heard the sound of a car pulling up behind the store and soon Elizabeth was coming through the door. The man who followed her was nothing like Keeley had imagined. She'd pictured him younger, knowing that he still participated in archaeological digs in remote and often dangerous places. But she guessed now that he was somewhere around Declan's age, in his early sixties, more Howard Carter than Sherlock Holmes, she thought, although this was no dusty desert explorer. He wore a dark business suit. His tie had some kind of crest, probably from a university or a club, she thought. Even after travelling all night he looked impeccable. He was a handsome, imposing man but he held back warily as he came into the room, ill at ease, glancing anxiously at them, his dark eyes resting on Luc in his RCMP uniform. Not a man comfortable with new social situations, thought Keeley.

Loki broke the ice, leaping up and walking over to Charles. "Welcome, Mr. Deeds, I'm Loki Andersson. I own the bookshop upstairs. You must be exhausted. Come and have some coffee."

Loki's friendliness and energy were impossible to resist, even for Charles Deeds.

"Thank you," he said, quietly. "Thank you. Please call me Charles. I'd enjoy a cup. It's been a long journey, but I had no choice but to come." Keeley couldn't place his accent. England, she thought or New England?

Luc stood up and extended his hand to Charles. "Corporal Luc Gagnon, RCMP," he said. "I'm the lead in this investigation." Charles nodded at him gravely.

"And I'm Keeley Carisbrooke," Keeley said, emerging from the trance of speculation that had held her in thrall since Charles walked in. "This is my shop."

Charles turned his dark eyes on her and she pulled herself together.

Loki pulled out a chair for Charles and they all sat down. Charles, restless and on edge, looked around the room. Once coffee had been poured Elizabeth spoke up. "Charles, you know why we asked you here. It's about the linen wrapped around Carter's book."

"Where is it? Where's the book? I must see it," Charles demanded. "That's why I'm here. For the book." He looked at Luc. "The report in the paper said you have it."

Luc answered, leaning forward, asserting his authority. "It's upstairs in Loki's safe. The newspaper report was intended to draw attention away from the store and avoid more incidents. I'm going to ask Loki to get it in a minute, but first, Mr. Deeds, we need to hear what you know about all this. There's clearly more going on here than a simple robbery attempt."

Charles shook his head, slowly. "I'm so sorry. I forget myself. This is so important to me…to my family. I trust Elizabeth implicitly but I was cautious of the rest of you. You're strangers. But it's clear that you are trustworthy too. You're Elizabeth's friends." He looked at Elizabeth with a smile that transformed his face. But it was quickly gone.

"I promise I'll tell you the whole story, everything I know, but please may I see the book? I believe it belonged to my grandfather, Joseph Deeds."

Keeley couldn't hide her surprise. "Your grandfather? Then you know its history, its provenance. How on earth did it find its way here?"

Luc stepped in again. "I'm sure we all have lots of questions but let's hear from Mr. Deeds first. Loki, would you get the book?"

Loki bounded out of the door and up the stairs. They waited for him in anxious silence. It didn't take him long. He put the book, still wrapped in the linen cloth, on the desk in front of Charles.

It seemed to Keeley, looking back, that time faltered in that moment. Everything moved in slow motion. Charles reached for the book, unwrapped it, gazed at it for a long time, wrapped it again, placed it gently back on the desk, put his head in his hands and shook uncontrollably as the tears ran down his face. This was so unexpected from such a reserved man that they all looked at each other, distressed and speechless, not knowing what to do.

Elizabeth leaned towards him and put her hand on his arm. "Charles," she said gently. "Charles, whatever it is, we can help you. Just tell us about it."

Slowly, Charles raised his head. Pain played across his face, mixed with extreme discomfort at having made such a public display of his emotions.

Loki stood up. "Charles, you haven't even had a chance to freshen up since your journey. What are we thinking? Let me show you the facilities and we'll wait for you. Take as long as you need." Charles looked up gratefully at Loki and got to his feet. Luc frowned and looked at Loki quizzically but Loki turned Charles away.

When Loki came back, Luc said, "He knows something, Loki. Maybe he knows who broke in here and attacked Declan. Don't let him off the hook. You've given him a chance to get his story straight now."

"I don't believe that Luc," said Elizabeth, firmly. "I've known him for years and I've never seen him like this. Give him a chance."

Luc nodded reluctantly but they could see he was on the alert, ready for anything now.

Charles came back after a few minutes, looking better. He stood beside his chair. "I'm so sorry. I don't know what came over me," he said. He looked at Luc. Something passed between them and Charles continued. "I must look guilty as hell in all of this. You need to know the whole story. I won't keep anything back. This is the first time in my life that I've ever told anyone. I didn't think there'd ever be a need."

Charles sat down and took the book in his hands again, unwrapping it and handing the linen cloth to Elizabeth.

"I'm sure this cloth is from ancient Egypt," he said, his voice growing stronger, his English accent deepening. "I'll subject it to radiocarbon dating but if it's connected to the tomb, I believe we'll find that it's 3,000 to 4,000 years old." Elizabeth gasped and put the cloth back on the desk.

Charles continued. "But the proof is in the provenance and that's my family story." He opened the cover of the book. "*The Tomb of Tut Ankh Amen, Volume One by Howard Carter and A.C. Mace*," he read. "It all starts here, with Howard Carter and the discovery of the tomb."

CHAPTER SIX

There was something disquieting about the silence that settled around them. Keeley looked at Loki for reassurance, but he was lost in his own thoughts. Have we called up danger from the long past? she thought. Have we summoned an ancient curse, reopened old wounds? She shook her head. She was being ridiculous.

Luc took out his notebook.

Charles's voice was soft again and they all leaned in towards him.

"My father, Edward Deeds, Teddy, was blind," Charles said. "He rarely spoke about his childhood. I know he was placed in an orphanage at some point until an older couple adopted him. He kept his name though and he knew his birth father's name—Joseph. Joseph Deeds. On his eighteenth birthday my father received from a solicitor some of Joseph's books and papers. This book was among them. His adoptive parents, who had told him nothing about his childhood, revealed then that his mother had died when he was three and Joseph, his father, who had looked after him alone after her death, had drowned when he was just six years old. Joseph had left everything to Teddy.

His adoptive parents had sold off Joseph's house and its contents and kept the funds in trust for him, according to Joseph's wishes."

Charles paused. Loki, sensing his distress asked, "Do you need some time, Charles? Another cup of coffee?"

Charles looked at him, appreciating the kindness. "Thank you, but I want to keep going."

Loki nodded, watchful.

"My father, Teddy, went on to live quite a reclusive life," said Charles. "He had the money from his father's trust fund and his adoptive parents left him well off. He continued to live in their house in upstate New York. His blindness was not a barrier to him. He was a scholar, specializing in ancient history and he was a prolific writer on the subject. He was helped in this endeavour by a series of assistants over the years.

"Then, when father was thirty-seven, a wonderful thing happened. A woman came to work for him, helping him with his manuscripts, cooking his meals and keeping him company. Kathleen was twelve years younger than Father. He was captivated by her Irish accent and her quick understanding of his areas of study. More than a typist, she contributed to his work, making it less dense, more readable and often, in conversation with her, he found himself thinking about his work in new ways. They fell in love and married."

Luc was scribbling furiously and Charles turned to him. "There's a lot more, Corporal Gagnon. Wouldn't you rather record it than write it?"

Luc met his gaze, clearly not convinced by this man or his storytelling.

"I'll keep writing, thanks," he said. "Writing helps me to concentrate on the important facts of the case."

The case, thought Keeley. It was a case. She'd almost forgotten, mesmerized by Charles's voice and his formal manner of speaking.

"Go on," said Luc.

Charles continued. "Five years after they were married, I was born. We lived in a place called Watertown, in Jefferson County, upstate New York." He looked around at them. "We were only thirty miles from Canada so this country has always felt familiar to me."

Keeley was still puzzled by his accent. She'd been sure it was English.

"We lived a quiet life, with books and music. Mother was a bright spark for us, keeping Father and me happy and safe. We were a close-knit family. When I was younger I asked my father a few times to tell me about his childhood, but he wouldn't say more than I've just told you. Perhaps that's all he knew.

"I grew up loving ancient history as they did, loving books and artifacts, loving scholarship and research. I often read to my father. He could read Braille, of course, and he listened to audio books but he loved it when I read to him. I learned that way, too and it deepened my interest in ancient times."

He put Carter's book on the table, caressed the cover with a feather-touch, gathered his thoughts.

"This is one of the books I read to him. I can't be sure yet, of course, because it was such a long time ago, but I'd like to have the chance to prove it."

They all looked at him, spellbound. He continued.

"When I was eighteen I was accepted into Cambridge University in England to study history and archaeology. Mother and Father were delighted and encouraged me, to the point where I managed to tear myself away from home and go across the Atlantic. I've lived in England for much of my life since then, but I visited them often. They are both gone now.

"When my father died my mother sent me some of his books and papers. It was some time before I felt strong enough to go through them. His loss was immense in my life. Carter's book was not among them but this was." Charles reached inside the jacket of his coat. Luc went on alert but Charles simply pulled an envelope from the inside pocket, opened it and took a letter out. "From my grandfather Joseph, to my father," said Charles. He started to read.

> *Teddy, my dear son, I don't know if you'll ever get this, but if it should find its way to you it means I am dead. I have given it—and a certain book— to my neighbour and asked him to give them to my solicitor, whom I have charged with finding you. The most important thing to tell you is that I love you more than life itself. After your mother died, you and I were alone for three years. You were only six when*

you were taken from me. The house where I am writing this is in Watertown, New York State. This house and all that's in it are yours. I pray that my solicitor is able to find you and convey this to you. I've asked that it be kept until you're of age, when you are better able to understand. I pray too, that those in whose care you find yourself are kind and loving. I blame myself for everything that happened and worst of all, I blame myself for your blindness. I was blind myself, in a different way—blind to the evil around me— and I cannot forgive myself that you were injured. My dearest little boy, I love you in this life and the next, wherever Anubis might send me. Teddy, when you are a grown man, if you want to know the whole story, I have written it for you, all that happened to us, every detail. It will not be easily found but I believe it will come to you if it is meant to. I have hidden it in the Tomb of Tut Ankh Amen. Your loving Father, Joseph.

Charles stopped reading and let his gaze rest on Keeley. "In the *Tomb of Tut Ankh Amen*. Do you understand? I always knew that he meant the book and not the tomb. The letter had been opened when I found it so I know my father had read it. It must have cut him to the core, such joy in knowing that his father had loved him and had not given him up willingly. Such pain in the loss. He must have decided then not to pass that pain along to me."

"The box of books…our box of books…" said Loki. "Your father's?"

"I believe so," said Charles. "When Mother moved to a smaller place after Father's death I got in touch with her to ask if I could have Carter's book. I hadn't read this letter then but I wanted something to remember him by. She told me that she'd boxed up his books with some of my magazines from university and asked one of Father's research colleagues to help her with an estate sale at the house. I thought at the time that the colleague had probably taken the books and found them a good home. It all seemed above board. I let it go then, happy in the thought that a library or a university had benefitted from Father's books and some of my periodicals. It was months before I read this letter and realized what was at stake. But no matter who I asked and where I looked I couldn't find Carter's book. It was lost to me."

"Until now," murmured Keeley.

Charles looked at her, appreciating her grasp of the situation. "Keeley, do you remember any of the other books in the box, anything about them?" he asked.

"I barely glimpsed them," she said.

Charles pursued it. "Was there, for instance, a series of magazines? The American Journal of Archaeology? They look like large paperback books, with royal blue covers. There should have been several of them."

It came back to her. "Yes!" she said. "I put them in a separate pile on my desk as I unpacked the box. They weren't taken. Loki has them."

"They are mine," said Charles. "You'll find my initials on the inside covers." He looked at Luc. "That box of books came from my parents' house in Watertown."

"I'll want you to check them for initials, Loki," said Luc. He leaned back and put down his notebook. "What's really going on here, Mr. Deeds? Why is someone so desperate to get their hands on this book that they'd commit violent robbery for it? And how on earth did it get here from upstate New York, or wherever it was?"

"I don't know," said Charles, a hint of anger and perplexity in his voice. "The last time I saw Carter's book and the magazines was in my parents' house. By the time I read my grandfather's letter, as I said, the book had left that house and gone out of my reach. I haven't thought about it for years. When Elizabeth phoned I was thunderstruck. I'm enough of a scientist to be skeptical. And superstitious enough to believe that the gods might be turning the wheel of fate."

Luc ignored the high-flown language and persisted. "Why would someone go to all this trouble to get the book, Mr. Deeds?"

Charles was frustrated and it showed. "I don't know. I've told you that. But I think the answer must lie in Carter's book, somehow."

He collected himself and steadied his voice. "I'm here to examine it, with your permission Corporal Gagnon, to put it under a kind of forensic scrutiny, to check every page and every word for a hidden code or message." Charles leaned towards Luc, pleading. "Will you let me do that, Corporal?"

Luc was silent. He looked down at his notebook, buying time. No one spoke. So many futures hung in the balance in that moment and they all realized it. When Luc finally spoke there was no mistaking the mistrust in his voice. "It's evidence," he said. "And Loki says it's probably valuable. We have no idea whether you're the rightful owner or not. Just because some of your old magazines were in the box we can't prove the whole thing belonged to you. What if someone else comes along to claim it?"

Charles shook his head and sighed in frustration and Luc relented slightly. "Although I admit you make a good case for it," he said.

Loki spoke up then. "Luc, I can help with this. I'll work with Charles to examine the book. It will never leave my sight and I'll keep it in my safe when we're not working on it. We can use the equipment at Folios. I have everything needed to handle and restore rare books, so it will come to no harm, even if someone else comes along to claim it."

Charles leapt up and shook Loki's hand. "Thank you. Thank you. That's more than generous."

The others were murmuring their approval of the plan. In the face of this, Luc conceded. "I'll hold you accountable Loki," he said. "As I said, it's evidence and must be thought of as such. Keep it safe."

"I will," said Loki.

"One more thing," said Luc, looking up at Charles, who was pacing anxiously round the room. "Who is Anubis? I've heard the name, of course, but I don't know why it's mentioned in your letter, Mr. Deeds."

Charles stood still. They waited. At last he spoke, quietly, his head bowed. "His name should not be used lightly…he is…" he faltered, then lifted his head to look at Luc and his voice gathered strength. "Anubis is one of Egypt's oldest gods. We first hear of him about 6,000 years BCE. We're all familiar with his image—the head of a jackal and the body of a man."

Luc persisted. "But what does this have to do with your grandfather?"

Charles went to the window and looked away into the distance, as if recalling another place and time, far away from the mountains and forests of Cascade Canyon.

"Anubis is the Lord of the Dead," he said.

There was something in the room Keeley could not define. Fear, perhaps. The glimpse of another world, strange and distant, where gods pulled the sun across the sky in the daytime and fought each other in the dark to bring the light back each morning; where every moment, every aspect of life was ruled by a god. Life and death. Anubis.

Charles turned and looked at them and spoke again, his voice hypnotic. "Anubis was present when it was decided whether or not a soul could enter the afterlife— we would think of it as heaven. He is often depicted in ancient drawings with a set of scales to weigh the human heart, where the soul lived. The scales of justice we're all so familiar with today outside our courtrooms, blind…" he stumbled but recovered quickly, "…they come from the scales of Anubis. When a soul came before Anubis for judgment, he checked the scales to make sure they were fair and balanced. Then he weighed the heart against the feather of Maat, the goddess of truth and justice. If the heart was good, it was lighter than the feather and the soul could enter a beautiful afterlife." He paused and turned back to the window, lost in thought.

Loki voiced what they were all thinking. "And if it was heavier than the feather?"

Charles did not look at him. "It was given to Ammit, the crocodile demon, to devour. It would wander the underworld in darkness forever, never finding peace."

Luc put his notebook down and went to stand next to Charles, who turned away from the window, shaking his head as if waking from a dream.

Elizabeth brought them back. "I can see why you're such a good teacher, Charles," she said. "You make it all so real."

Too real, thought Keeley. She knew that scales and feathers and demons would haunt her dreams.

Luc looked round at them all. "I'd like to keep this between us for now, the things Mr. Deeds has told us and the fact that we're examining the book." He saw the consternation in Keeley's face.

"Keeley, just tell the students and Rory and Declan that Mr. Deeds is examining the book because he's an expert. But nothing else. Nothing about his father's letter. Not yet."

They all agreed.

Elizabeth put her hand on Charles's arm. "Charles, let me take you to the hotel. We can meet for dinner if you like or if you'd just like to rest, that's fine too." Charles nodded gratefully.

Loki picked up the book and wrapped it in the linen. "I'll take this back up to my safe," he said. "When would you like to start on this, Charles?"

"Can we start tomorrow?" asked Charles. "If you can spare the time, that is. I know what an intrusion this is into all your lives."

"Tomorrow it is!" said Loki. "I'll pick you up at your hotel at nine. We can grab some breakfast next door before we start."

"Thank you, all of you. I'll see you tomorrow," said Charles. With a long glance at the book in Loki's hands, he left with Elizabeth. Luc walked them out.

Keeley and Loki sat for a moment, looking at each other. "What a story," said Loki. "What a mystery."

Keeley nodded. "I know. We've stumbled into a secret that might go all the way back to Tutankhamun. I can't help thinking that the first people who stumbled into it, Carter and Carnarvon, were plagued by rumours of a curse. Have we just brought it all back to life?"

CHAPTER SEVEN

Keeley was at her desk in the morning when Charles and Loki came in. "Join us for breakfast, Keeley?" asked Loki.

Charles smiled at her. She could see that he was rested and much more relaxed than he had been the previous day. She was struck again by the way the smile transformed his face.

"Hello, you two," she said. "I wish I could but I have a mountain of paperwork. Will you be taking a lunch break?"

Charles spoke up. "Oh yes, we will indeed," he said. "It would be my pleasure to take you both out for lunch."

They settled on a time and Loki and Charles headed to Bean Cabin for breakfast. As they walked away Keeley could hear them talking warmly and laughing occasionally. This is a strange way to meet someone, she thought, suddenly realizing that she already hoped Charles would become their friend.

At lunchtime they came downstairs from Folios to meet her. They were in animated conversation about the types of printing presses and binderies used in the 1920s.

"We've invented a cover story," Loki said to her, enthusiastically. "We're telling everyone that Charles is visiting the University of BC to look at some of their first folios and manuscripts. They have a world-class collection. And we're saying that someone at the university suggested he visit my bookshop and now I've asked him to consult with me on some of my rare books. It's a bit of a stretch but only someone with an ulterior motive would question it."

"Have you told Luc?" asked Keeley.

"The cautious Corporal Gagnon agrees with it," said Charles with a wry smile.

They went next door to Bean Cabin and were met with curious looks from everyone there. Charles was wearing a Harris Tweed jacket with a woollen scarf twisted casually round his neck. He looked like a model for Country Life magazine. He might as well have carried a sign that said, 'Professor from England'.

Loki and Charles didn't notice the looks. They were debating the merits of various type fonts. Keeley looked round the café and tried to smile convincingly at everyone. Yvonne and Peter hurried over.

"Hello again, Charles," Yvonne said. "We're so happy you came back to us for lunch."

Peter unexpectedly reached out and shook Charles's hand. Charles was clearly surprised. Keeley hadn't told Yvonne and Peter about the real reason for Charles's visit. She'd desperately wanted to, but Luc had insisted. But they were among her oldest friends and they suspected that Charles's arrival had something to do with the book and the break-in.

"You've all made me so welcome," Charles said. "It's such a lovely village."

"Whatever it is you're doing here," said Peter in a low voice, "we just want to make sure everyone stays safe." Peter was a big man. There was no threat in his voice, but the unspoken concern was loud and clear.

"I would never knowingly bring harm into the lives of these dear people," Charles answered quietly. "They are fortunate to have such a good friend in you."

Peter gave Charles a long look. Then suddenly something shifted. He beamed at Charles. He'd decided to trust him and once that bridge was crossed, the moment was over.

"Cream horns for dessert then," he said cheerfully, and went off to the kitchen.

Over hearty vegetable soup and deli sandwiches Keeley, Loki and Charles made small talk. A few curious villagers stopped by to say hello, to scrutinize Charles and try to get some tidbit of information they could gossip about at the pub or the grocery store. But Charles was a master of dissembling. He was charming, open, and friendly, and above all he stuck unwaveringly to the cover story.

After cream horns, declared by Charles to be the best he'd ever tasted, they walked back to Past Life.

"It's only a matter of time until the whole village knows you're here," said Loki. "Makes me wonder if whoever came after the book will put two and two together."

Keeley was startled and instantly afraid. "Rory and Arwen are alone in the store," she said. "We should call

Luc. You think the people who did this will come back?"
There was panic in her voice.

Loki quickly took her hand. "They'll never try anything in the daytime," he said, "but I do think we should
have another meeting with Luc, all of us who know about
this, so we can be proactive about what might happen."

Charles looked worried. "I should not have come," he
said. "I've put you all in danger. If anything happens I'll
never forgive myself. Shall I leave?"

"No Charles, this wasn't your fault," said Keeley,
firmly. "You were on the other side of the world when the
break-in and the attack on Declan happened. Someone is
responsible for this and we'll never find out who without
your help. And it's about your birthright, Charles. We all
want to see it through."

Charles nodded. "Yes, of course, you're right," he said.
"The sooner we find some answers the safer we'll all
be." He glanced back at Bean Cabin and smiled. "And I
wouldn't want to cross Peter after promising him you'll all
be safe."

The three of them spent a long time in conversation,
standing just outside the back door of Past Life, out of
earshot of curious listeners. After they'd come to an agreement they all went back to work.

Keeley made some calls.

By six o'clock Keeley, Loki and Charles were walking
up the front steps of Rory's and Declan's house. Rory
greeted them at the front door. Arwen was already inside
with Scott and Sherine. Keeley had decided that they all
needed to be given the whole story and had called Luc

to discuss it with him. He'd agreed reluctantly, so Keeley had contacted the students and Rory and Declan and told them about Charles's family connection to the book and his search for the clues it might contain.

Declan sat in a deeply cushioned leather chair beside the glowing fireplace. He was looking much better and was clearly happy to be included. Keeley made introductions and Rory motioned them all to sit down. Charles immediately went to sit beside Declan and spoke in low tones to him. Declan nodded, put his hand reassuringly on Charles's arm and Charles sat back, relief on his face.

Knowing Charles even for this short time, Keeley felt sure he'd apologized to Declan for the attack. They were quite similar in many ways, she thought, quiet scholars content with dusty books, artifacts and music. She imagined they'd have lots to talk about once this was over.

Rory went to the kitchen and came back with a tray of wine glasses. Sherine and Scott followed with plates of finger food. They were all telling Charles about the delights of Cascade Canyon when a knock on the door announced Luc Gagnon. There was nothing unusual in Luc coming to see Declan as a follow-up to the attack so he'd come in uniform, in the squad car. He dropped gratefully into a chair, nodded hello to everyone and accepted a mug of hot chocolate from Arwen.

"What's up?" he asked. "Loki, I think you called this meeting?"

Loki was quiet for a moment and they all looked at him expectantly. They were relaxed, enjoying each other's company, and the students were excited about being included in the conversations.

"I think we're all in danger," said Loki.

The atmosphere in the room became electric. Declan looked at Rory, fear in his eyes, Keeley and Charles exchanged a glance, understanding what Loki was talking about, but the others looked at Loki in alarm. Luc put his mug of hot chocolate down and sat up straight.

"I'm sorry everyone," said Loki, "perhaps I should have said that differently but it's what I…we..." he included Charles and Keeley in his gesture, "…what we think. We were in Bean Cabin today and it seemed like the whole village came over to check out Charles. By now the word is out that he's here. We think our cover story is strong but whoever did this will put two and two together and we think they might try again to get the book or get information," he paused, looking at Declan with sympathy and anxiety playing across his face, "by any means."

Luc pulled his radio out of his belt. "Dispatch, send a patrol car to Past Life Emporium in Cascade Canyon. Drive by every half hour."

In an instant, everything had changed. They waited for Luc to finish then they all started talking at once.

Luc held up his hands. "Hold it! Hold it everyone. Let's talk about this. I have some ideas." He gave Charles a hard look. "And they start with you leaving town."

All the sadness and reserve Keeley had seen when they'd first met came back to Charles's face. He was on his guard.

"I've offered to do that," he said in a cold, detached voice. "It was the first thing I did when we realized there was still danger. If you think I must leave I'll go immediately."

Luc was surprised by the change in Charles. He'd been cautious of Charles's charm and sympathetic character. Somehow hearing the cool, formal note in Charles's voice gave Luc pause. Maybe he wasn't a fraud after all. Or he would have kept up the charade.

Keeley was upset. She felt protective towards Charles for reasons she couldn't clearly identify, perhaps the sadness of his family story, perhaps because he seemed so alone.

"I think that's a mistake, Luc," she said emphatically. "Loki agrees with me. We'll get to the bottom of things much faster with Charles's help. Otherwise we're just wandering around in the dark. Then we'd have to hand all this over to outside investigators, maybe even Interpol."

The mention of Interpol had Luc's attention. He wanted his own police force to solve the crime that had impacted his community and his friends so deeply.

He relented. "I'm willing to listen to ideas," he said. "And I'm willing to give you the benefit of the doubt, Mr. Deeds, because these good people, who I know and trust, seem to be vouching for you."

This did nothing to make Charles lower his guard. He sat in the chair next to Declan, contained, withdrawn, watchful.

Declan spoke for the first time. "I hope you'll understand, all of you, that I desperately want to catch the fellow who did this to me and to all of us. I don't want anyone else to go through this…" he tapered off and Arwen, sitting on the floor beside him, reached for his hand. Declan continued. "But I've always had an instinct about people and I have an instinct about this man here." He looked at Charles. "I'm sure we can trust him. I just feel that."

Charles looked back at him and all his reserve and detachment crumbled.

"That means more to me than anything else could, coming from you, who suffered the most harm from this," Charles said. His voice faltered but he found strength. "Thank you."

Declan smiled at Charles. "I've heard your mother was Irish, Charles," he said.

"She was," said Charles. "I hold dual citizenship—Irish and American."

"Sure, that's enough for me!" declared Declan. "We're practically related!"

They all laughed and the tension dissolved.

Luc pressed on, eager to move into a more pragmatic discussion. "Are you making progress with the forensic study of the book, Mr. Deeds?" he asked.

Loki answered. "Slowly, very slowly. It's going to take time. But that's not why we asked everyone here. We have a plan."

Luc raised his eyebrows. "A plan? What plan?" he said.

Keeley answered him. "We're going to set a trap."

CHAPTER EIGHT

Luc was on his feet. "You will do no such thing!" he said. "You'll leave this to us. We've just been talking about the possibility of the bad guys coming back for a second try. They must be getting more and more desperate. Someone will get hurt. One of you will get hurt. Just put that idea out of your heads." He paced around, stressed by the thought of them taking this into their own hands.

Keeley tried to calm him down. "Luc, I should have eased into the trap thing. We'd never do this without the backup of the police. But we have thought about it. At least let us explain our idea to you. Then, if you're still opposed, we'll drop it."

Loki started to object but she silenced him with a look. Better to have Luc on their side.

"Charles," she said. "Would you explain to Luc and to everyone else what we talked about earlier?" She wanted Charles back inside their circle instead of outside and hoped this would do it.

"Corporal Gagnon," said Charles, steadily. "I'm sorry I reacted badly earlier. You're just doing your job and I respect that. Complicating things, these people are your friends and you have no reason at all to trust me, although I imagine you've already looked me up in every possible system." He raised his eyebrows at Luc, who gave a firm nod.

Charles continued. "As you know, we believe the book and the clues or messages it contains are the key to all of this. It's the book they're after. So let's give it to them."

Everyone except Keeley and Loki looked at him in surprise.

He continued quickly. "Not actually give it to them, of course, but let them think it's within easy reach. I'll do an interview with the local paper, telling them that I'm here to evaluate Carter's book. I'll let it be known that I'm working with Loki at Forest Folios to do this and that the police have now returned the book to Folios so I can study it."

Luc nodded slowly. So far he was with them.

"The trap is this," said Charles. "I'll work there alone at night, lights on. I'll be visible through the Folios windows from the woods at the back."

Luc and some of the others began to protest but Charles carried on. "Corporal Gagnon, your patrol car will come past every half hour. The officers will stop, come around to the back, call up the steps to me and I will come to the door of Folios to answer them. Anyone watching this from the woods will soon get an idea of the routine and realize that between patrols there is time to for them to get the book—and me too, perhaps." He said this almost serenely, in sharp contrast to his words. He was talking about putting his safety, perhaps his life, at risk.

THE SCALES OF ANUBIS

But Luc was beginning to see the plan. "But you wouldn't really be alone up in Folios, would you, Mr. Deeds? A couple of my officers would be up there with you. So if anyone tried anything we'd be there to get them."

"Exactly, Corporal Gagnon!" said Charles. "Exactly. No one else need be involved. The staff at Past Life—and Loki too—would have gone home before dark and in a group."

Loki protested. "Not happening," he said. "I'm going to be there. I don't care how many police officers are up there, it's my bookshop and I'm going to be there to see this through."

Charles, who'd known he couldn't keep Loki away, had just been using him to press his case to Luc.

Scott piped up. "I think I can help too," he said. "I can stand guard out in the woods or something."

Sherine turned shining eyes on him.

But Charles shook his head vehemently. "No, absolutely not. No one else is to be put in harm's way. I know I can't stop you from being there, Loki, but the plan will fail if too many of us try to help." He looked at Luc, waiting for his response.

Luc took his time. He paced around the room a bit more, wrote down a couple of things in his notebook and said, at last. "I'm willing to give this a try on condition that no one other than Mr. Deeds and Loki are involved. Everyone else has to stay far away from there."

"Thank God," said Declan, fervently. They knew what he meant. Keeley and the students, as well as Rory, would stay safe.

While Rory and Arwen went to get more snacks, the rest of them chatted. They were excited, animated. It was almost like a game or a mystery plot, thought Keeley, except that it was real and there were lives on the line.

They went over the plan in fine detail, taking their lead from Luc, who knew more about bad guys and stake-outs than any of them. It was agreed that Loki and Charles would call the local paper, The Cascade Courier, the next day and give them an interview.

"When do they publish?" Charles asked. "Are they weekly?"

"Twice weekly," said Keeley. "The interview will go in the Friday edition. It will go up on their website too, so anyone searching will find the reference immediately. Whoever is looking for this book has been searching the web. They probably have a system to alert them to any new reference to it. I'm sure that's how they were able to find the book so quickly after Scott's social media posts."

"Then we start Friday night?" asked Charles.

"Saturday," said Luc. "That will give me time to put the surveillance team in place. Two officers in the patrol car, two in the woods and two more somewhere in Loki's shop where they can't be seen from outside. There are lots of people around in the daytime on Saturday so whoever is coming for the book will wait until evening. Safer all round. I'll put a conspicuous watch on Folios until then."

"How will the police officers get to up to Loki's without being seen?" asked Sherine. Everyone looked at her in surprise. She was a sweet person, kind and gentle, quiet and shy, studying nursing at university. Sherine rarely spoke when there were strangers present. But the whole idea of Scott being heroic seemed to have given her confidence.

"Good question, Sherine," said Luc. "We'll need to get them up there inconspicuously."

"I have a kitchen and a bathroom up in the shop," said Loki. "If they come up earlier in the day, in civvies, pretending to be customers, they can hide out in the back."

"I could come in with them," Sherine spoke up again. Everyone was astonished. "It will look more natural if there's a group of us."

Scott looked doubtful but Luc saw no danger.

"That would be great Sherine," he said. "I'll send them to Past Life at about four o'clock in the afternoon. Can you be there then?"

"Yes," she said. "Scott and I always work there on weekends." Scott looked at her proudly.

"I'll come in on Saturday too, to cover Past Life while Sherine takes the officers upstairs," said Arwen.

"We'll do this for two days," said Luc. "It's a lot of staff hours on our side and I think if they haven't tried anything by then, we're barking up the wrong tree. We'll repeat the plan on Sunday. I'll switch the officers in the woods with the ones in the bookshop so if someone's keeping watch they won't recognize them. Everyone OK with that?"

It was agreed. Everyone had a part to play. The plan was outlined in great detail.

It seemed foolproof, thought Keeley. But what was it Robbie Burns said about the best-laid schemes often going awry?

CHAPTER NINE

Keeley and Arwen were having lunch at Bean Cabin when the Friday newspapers were delivered. Arwen went over to the counter to get one and they didn't have to look very hard to find their article. There on the front page was the interview with Charles with one of Scott's photos of the book, a photo of the box and a photo of Charles looking very handsome and scholarly. The caption read *Professor Charles Deeds, University College, London.*

Keeley smiled at Arwen. "A few hearts will be beating faster when they see that," she observed.

"No kidding!" said Arwen. "He's gorgeous. I know he's almost old enough to be my grandfather but he's so handsome and mysterious. If I was twenty years older…" she teased.

"Like me, you mean?" laughed Keeley.

Arwen smiled at her. "I know your heart lies with a certain mountaineer. One of these days you two will go public. Everyone knows, you know."

"Then they know more than we do," said Keeley. "We're still trying to figure it out, just taking it slowly. You know

I haven't been with anyone since we lost your dad." Tears filled her eyes and Arwen took her hand.

"I know Mum, but it's been six years now," she said, softly, "and Loki is a great guy."

Keeley smiled at her and they turned their attention back to the newspaper article. Charles had done exactly what they'd planned.

Courier: Mr. Deeds, you contacted us to let us know that you're here to help appraise the book that seems to be at the centre of the break-in at Past Life second-hand shop. Why did you feel the need to go public with your presence here?

Deeds: Well, I get asked about it at every turn here, on the street, in the café. Everyone's so interested. I live in a little English village so I understand the curiosity and closeness of village life. I thought it would be simpler just to tell everyone at once, through your well-read newspaper.

Courier: We are a curious bunch here in Cascade Canyon. Glad you came to our paper, Mr. Deeds. Tell us more about how you happened to get involved in this.

Deeds: I'm actually here in BC to do some consulting at the University of British Columbia. After finding out through a mutual friend that I was in town, Mr. Andresson from Forest Folios contacted me to seek my opinion on The Tomb of Tut Ankh Amen, Volume One by Howard Carter. I was happy to help, of course, but when I heard that the book was the target of a break-in at the second-hand shop and the unfortunate injury inflicted on one of their staff I became deeply curious about why this book is so sought-after. And why someone would just leave it in a box of books on the doorstep of Past Life. It's valuable in itself, certainly, but I wonder if there isn't another reason someone wants to get their hands on it. With its Egyptian connections it could be concealing anything, perhaps even the clues to finding another tomb. As a student of ancient history, I couldn't pass up the chance to examine it.

Courier: And what qualifies you to do that?

Deeds: I'm an historian and an archaeologist. One of my areas of expertise is ancient Egypt and while pursuing my own interest in this area I've also become an expert on rare books about Egypt, particularly those published in the early twentieth century.

Courier: Well it sounds as if they have the right person to figure out this mystery. I imagine it will take quite a bit of time, though. How long will you be here in BC, Mr. Deeds?

Deeds: Well that's the problem, actually. I'm due back in London in three days. So I'm working pretty much round the clock.

Courier: At the RCMP precinct? Corporal Gagnon told us they'd taken the book there for safekeeping.

Deeds: No, they're going to release it back to Mr. Andresson and myself on Saturday. (Ed. the day after this edition.) We'll be working at Forest Folios. All the specialized equipment is there and the police will do their best to keep an eye on the store. My job is to thoroughly examine the book, so I'm just concentrating on that. Perhaps I'll discover something and perhaps I won't. But I'll be able to give Mr. Andresson a proper valuation and maybe find a clue that will help the police with their enquiries.

Keeley put the paper down. She looked around Bean Cabin and noticed that quite a few people were also looking at the paper and making surreptitious glances towards their table.

"That will definitely do the trick," she said to Arwen. "Word will spread like wildfire around the village, but most important of all, Charles used several key words and phrases—his own name, the full name of the book and all the details of where and when he and Loki will be working on it. If anyone's searching the web using any of those terms they'll find this article right away."

Arwen looked unhappy. "Mum, do you think they'll be OK, Loki and Charles?" she asked. "And what about the rest of us?"

Keeley looked at her daughter and said, with all the confidence she could muster, "I know it's hard, love, but I honestly think it's the only way to solve this. Otherwise Charles will leave and we'll still be at the mercy of whoever's out there."

Arwen shivered and Keeley went on quickly. "And we have Luc of course, and all the members of his team. I trust them absolutely or I wouldn't have agreed to this. We just have to do our part and stay together in a group, whether we're here in the village, at home or the three of you in the residence. It should all be over soon."

Arwen brightened. "Let's have dinner together at our place tonight, Mum, all of us. We can order pizza and we can ask Rory if Declan's well enough to come, even for a little while. That will help everyone, I think."

"Great idea!" said Keeley. "You sort out pizza and I'll call Rory," she said. "Before we leave I'll get some of Peter's pastries for dessert."

After lunch they went back to Past Life, which was filled with customers. Scott and Sherine were looking after the store while Rory took a rare day off to spend time with Declan. Loki and Charles were upstairs in Folios. Keeley saw several new boxes of donations containing records and CDs. She picked up the phone to call Rory about dinner. Rory said he wouldn't be able to keep Declan away but they would just come for a little while.

"Tell Declan I have some music for him to look through," said Keeley. "I'll bring the records and CDs this evening and you can take them home with you."

She phoned upstairs to Folios and got Loki, who promised he and Charles would be there. Keeley knew Charles was in Folios kitchen working on Carter's book, out of sight of any inquisitive patrons.

"You'd be amazed how many people are asking about it," Loki told Keeley. "I'm giving them the same story Charles gave the newspaper. Seems to be working."

At six o'clock they closed up Past Life and headed to Keeley's house. They all travelled together in Keeley's faithful old Mini Cooper, Scott and Sherine happily huddled in the back and Arwen in the front with Keeley.

Keeley's house was nestled against the forest, about ten minutes' drive from Past Life. On good days she walked, but in the present circumstances it was safer to drive. The house was more than a hundred years old, in the craftsman style, with a huge covered porch running the full length of the front and a peaked roof on the second floor. It was too big for Keeley but she couldn't bear to give it up. Arwen often stayed over when she wasn't in the student residence at the university and Sherine stayed too, when Arwen was there. That meant Scott was a frequent visitor. Peter and Yvonne lived a few houses away. Loki often stopped by on his way back from an evening hike and they all loved to hang out together on the front porch in summer or relax in front of the huge fireplace in winter. It wasn't unusual to find Rory whipping up something delicious in the kitchen while Declan took care of the music. To Keeley it was the perfect home, huge and rambling, warm and cozy and often filled with family and friends.

They all piled into the house and went to get things ready for dinner. Keeley had a massive old oak refectory table she'd bought from a shipment of English antiques. It had several boards to extend its length and could easily seat twelve. By the time the fire was crackling in the hearth and the table was set, Loki and Charles had arrived. The doorbell announced pizza and Keeley opened the door to see that right behind the pizza van, Rory was helping Declan get out of their car.

Charles had been watching for them. He slipped past Keeley and rushed to support Declan, so with Rory on one side and Charles on the other, Declan made his way slowly and steadily up the front steps. Once in the house Declan assured everyone that he was well enough to sit at the table. In the way they'd now become used to, everyone looked at Rory for confirmation. Rory nodded his approval and Declan laughed a happy laugh that sent their spirits soaring. "Sure, the man will never let me forget this," he said, smiling at Rory. "He'll be bossing me around until kingdom come."

"You're lucky to have me taking charge," said Rory, imperiously. "Look what you get up to when you're left to your own devices." He laughed and they all tucked into the pizza with gusto.

They were relishing the pastries when Loki suddenly said, "Tell them, Charles."

Chatter stopped instantly. All eyes were on Charles, who looked round the table and finally turned his intense gaze on Keeley.

"I found something," he said.

CHAPTER TEN

Keeley was the first to find her voice. "What did you say, Charles? You found something? In the book?"

Charles nodded, stood up from the table and walked over to pick up his battered leather satchel. He took out a cloth book bag and came back to stand by the table. Carefully clearing the place in front of him he reached into the bag and took out Carter's book.

"So that's it," said Declan softly. "There it is. The reason for all of this."

"This is it, Declan," said Charles. "You have my word that I'll get to the bottom of this before I leave. I can't bear the thought that you were hurt because of this. We'll get the person who did this to you, I promise."

Declan shook his head. "Don't you be putting yourself at risk for this, Charles. It's not what I want, not what any of us wants."

"I won't. But I want them to pay for what they did to you," Charles said, the threat in his voice so unlike anything they'd heard from him before that they were all surprised. He recovered quickly. "But let me show you what I've found. Not quite there yet, but it's a step forward."

He sat down again, placed the book on the table and opened the cover to reveal the images there. It took Keeley back to the moment she and Loki had first opened the book.

"What does it mean?" asked Sherine.

"They are cartouches, shapes that holds the symbols of a royal name," Charles explained. "Egyptian kings had five names. One of them was their given name at birth, although Tutankhamun changed his at some point, and the other four they were given when they took the throne. Cartouches only represent the two most important names. The one on the left here says 'Tutankhamun, ruler of Upper Heliopolis.' Tutankhamun was his given name. The cartouche on the right is one of his throne names—'Nebkheperura.'"

"So we're wrong when we call him King Tut," said Sherine. "He was really King Neb…whatever you said."

"No," Charles went on, "he was King Tutankhamun. The other names were spiritual and symbolic, representing his power."

Sherine had another question. "Why is his name spelled like that on the book? We spell it differently don't we?"

"You'll find several different spellings in documents and history books," said Charles. "But we've generally settled on Tutankhamun." He spelled it out.

Rory couldn't wait any longer. "What is it you've found Charles? Please don't keep us in suspense."

Charles lifted the open book and held it up to them at eye level. "It's hard to tell just by looking at it, but the back cover is thicker than the front cover."

"That's it?" said Scott, disappointed. "I thought we'd find a map of a new tomb."

"There something more," said Charles, "but first I should say that the new tomb possibility was mainly for the newspaper. That's not what we're expecting to find here, although we might find something to lead us to artifacts."

He ran his finger along the rim of the cover. "I've looked at this under a special light and I can see that there's something inside. Paper, perhaps a letter. Loki agrees with me."

"Wow," said Scott. "Take it out and let's read it!"

Charles laughed at his enthusiasm. "I will, Scott," he said. "But I must protect the book while I'm doing it. I'll start work on it tomorrow. Loki has the tools I need, but it will take time. We'll want to restore the cover as soon as I've removed whatever is inside but I should be able to get it done by tomorrow evening, I hope."

"That's amazing!" said Arwen. "So exciting!"

Rory raised his glass to Charles. "Here's to you, our new friend, who happens to be the genius we need right at this moment."

Charles shook his head in good-natured disagreement but they'd all picked up their glasses for the toast.

Loki echoed Rory. "To Charles, our resident genius and best of all, our new friend."

Charles was clearly moved. He struggled to speak but gave up. Instead he picked up Carter's book, looked at it for a long time, put it back in the book bag and took it over to safely store it in his leather satchel.

Keeley watched him. The stakes are really high for him, she thought. This is his family history, his family mystery. I hope he finds the answers he needs.

"I think I'll head back over to Folios and do more work on this," said Charles. "Thanks for everything you've all done. Thanks especially for calling me a friend. There are very few people in this world I call friends. It's an honour for me to be counted among yours."

He picked up the satchel and walked to the door. Loki leapt up to go with him. "I'll drive you to Folios and then to the hotel," he said.

"We'll leave the book in Loki's safe again tonight," said Charles. "No one will have any idea that I'm there so they won't come looking for it. They'll expect Corporal Gagnon to deliver it to us at Folios tomorrow. He's going to make a big show of doing just that, part of the trap of course."

"See you all tomorrow," said Charles. "Especially this young lady," he nodded at Sherine and she smiled shyly back at him, "who'll be bravely bringing the officers up to Folios."

Scott looked at Charles with something like hero worship in his eyes.

Loki and Charles headed for the door. Charles had his satchel firmly across his shoulder and was holding on with both hands.

"We should go too," said Rory, and Declan nodded gratefully. Leaning on Rory and Scott, Declan made his way to the car and soon they were on their way. Rory was giving Scott a ride home to the university, part of their plan to keep an eye on each other.

Arwen and Sherine were staying with Keeley. They'd done it so often that Sherine kept an overnight bag and a change of clothes in the spare room. Arwen still had her old room. The two girls insisted on cleaning up after dinner. Keeley could hear them laughing and chatting in the kitchen and soon there were goodnight hugs all round. Keeley knew they'd talk in Arwen's room long into the night.

She turned the lights down, lit some candles and threw another log on the fire. Then she poured herself a glass of wine, sank into a soft wing chair and gazed into the flames.

So many questions, she thought. Was this a straight line back to the fabled Howard Carter and even further, to the legend of King Tutankhamun? Or was it a new, twisted story, slithering through recent history and lying in wait for them, like a cobra poised to strike.

CHAPTER ELEVEN

Keeley and the students had just opened Past Life on Saturday morning when Mr. and Mrs. Ito hurried in and came straight to the desk. They were a much-loved couple, a central part of the community. Mr. Ito, Kaito, was a world-renowned ceramicist.

"Keeley, we must speak to you privately," said Mrs. Ito. She was out of breath and Keeley realized with a start that she and her husband, who had always seemed ageless and so full of life, were feeling the passing of the years.

"Would you like to come to the back room and sit down?" she asked. "And would you like tea?"

They nodded gratefully and followed her back.

"Arwen, would you get tea for Mr. and Mrs. Ito please?" Keeley asked her daughter, who came with them to the back room, quickly organized tea and returned to the front of the store.

While Mr. Ito sipped his tea, Mrs. Ito talked to Keeley, her soft, musical voice urgent with information. "Keeley, the box of books came from us."

Keeley was speechless. She wondered whether to call Luc, but decided that the Itos were already upset enough and she would just do her best to calm and restore them. She had so many questions but gathered her patience and simply said, "Please tell me about it."

Mrs. Ito was clearly distressed. "I'm so afraid we've done something wrong but we can't see how. We were reading yesterday's newspaper this morning at breakfast and when Mr. Ito saw the interview with Mr. Deeds and the photo of the box we knew we had to come over right away."

"I'm sure you haven't done anything wrong," said Keeley, gently. "In fact, this is the best thing that could possibly happen. This is going to be so much help to us and to Corporal Gagnon."

She watched as they brightened and looked at each other with relief. "Well, if we can help we'll do anything we can," said Mrs. Ito. "We know Declan so well. He always finds the perfect music for Mr. Ito to listen to when he is making his pottery. Please tell him we send him our best wishes."

"I will," said Keeley. "He's much better. We hope to have him back here soon." She paused, not wanting to make them more anxious. "How would you feel about me phoning Loki and Charles, Charles Deeds, and asking them to come down? They're upstairs in Folios."

Mrs. Ito looked at her husband who nodded once, his serious eyes never leaving his wife's face.

"If you think that's the best thing, Keeley," Mrs. Ito said. "We don't mind at all."

Keeley refilled their tea and phoned up to Folios. Within minutes Charles and Loki arrived.

"I've locked up," said Loki, entering the room at speed, as usual. "It's fine. We're not due to open for another hour."

Charles, behind him, was carrying the book bag. He saw the Itos and walked slowly over to where they sat. He bowed first to Mrs. Ito then turned to Mr. Ito and bowed again. "Mr. Ito," he said with deep respect. "It's my honour to meet you and your wife. I'm a great admirer of your work. In fact, I own several pieces."

Mr. Ito's face lit up with pleasure. "Thank you Mr. Deeds. The honour is mine."

An air of calm entered the room as Loki and Charles pulled up chairs, helped themselves to tea and waited respectfully for the Itos to speak. Mrs. Ito, feeling at ease now, began.

"Our grandson dropped off the box of books. He's a very good grandson who helps us a lot even though he's in university now."

Mr. Ito nodded quickly in agreement. "A very good grandson," he echoed.

Mrs. Ito continued. "He was supposed to take it up to your shop, Loki, but by the time he got here everything was closed and he thought it would be safer at the front door than in the back lane. He knew it would make its way to you eventually."

"He's right," said Keeley. "I always ask Loki to have a look at the old books we get."

Charles spoke quietly, his dark eyes on the Itos. "How wonderful to have such a good grandson," he said. "And he's part of the story of the book now. I think he will be pleased, as most young people love adventure and mystery." Very gently, he had steered Mrs. Ito back to her story.

"He will be surprised when he hears all of this," she said. "But I will tell you more. There is much more to be told about how the box of books came to us."

At last, thought Keeley. At last the puzzle pieces were coming together.

"Our story starts many years ago, in the 1980s," Mrs. Ito said, her voice gathering strength and confidence. "My husband was a guest professor at the New York State College of Ceramics at Alfred University. It was such a happy time in our lives. My husband was teaching, which he loves, and I was writing articles about life in the United States for Japanese publications. We had two young sons who were in English language school. When we finally moved from Japan to Cascade Canyon ten years ago we were following our sons, who learned to love North America during our time in New York."

Charles spoke again. "You've given them the best of both worlds," he said.

Mr. Ito spoke. "I believe we have," he said. "Here in Canada they feel both fully Canadian and fully Japanese. Our grandson has just finished his undergraduate degree at the University of British Columbia. In fact, Mr. Deeds, our grandson is an archaeologist."

"The best profession in the world!" Charles declared, smiling. "What's he working on?"

Mr. Ito looked delighted to have been asked. "Near here, hidden deep in the forest, there's evidence of a lost community of Japanese settlers from the early part of the twentieth century. It was laid out in the traditional Japanese way with a communal bath house, gardens and even a shrine. It's the only discovery of its kind in North America. Our grandson worked on that project for two years," he said proudly. "The dig is completed now, but there's so much more research to be done."

"I've read about it in one of my journals," said Charles. "Weren't there some lovely ceramics found?"

"Yes, many lovely bowls," said Mr. Ito. He sighed. "It was as if people had just walked out and left their homes, which of course, they had. In 1942, Japanese Canadians, even those who had been here for generations, had their property seized and were sent to internment camps. So the forest reclaimed their village and kept it secret for eighty years."

Silence fell on the group. Suddenly the story of the box of books was overtaken by immense human tragedy and loss.

Mr. Ito understood their sorrow at past injustices.

"There is a Japanese proverb," he said. " 'Wherever you live, you come to love it.' This is so true for my family. This is our home, our children's home, our grand-children's home. This is our village now."

"Yes," said Keeley. No other words were needed.

Mrs. Ito looked at her husband. "We've travelled a long way from New York, haven't we?" She looked round the table. "Let me tell you more about the box of books."

A special moment had passed but would not be forgotten. Mrs. Ito continued. "We were at the College of Ceramics for two years. During that time, because we knew we would be going back to Japan, we spent every weekend exploring the towns and countryside near us in New York state. We often collected antiques—pottery and ceramics mainly. We would try to stay in a different town each weekend. One of these trips took us to a town in Jefferson County, called Watertown."

Charles gasped. "I was born there," he said. He steadied himself by taking a sip of tea, his eyes fixed on Mrs. Ito.

The Itos looked at him in surprise and Keeley realized that they knew nothing of the real reason for Charles being there. They'd only seen the newspaper article. But Mrs. Ito seemed to understand immediately. "Then this is where our story becomes yours," she said. "While we were in Watertown we heard of an estate sale at a house nearby. The woman there was elderly and…" she looked at Charles. "Could she have been a family member of yours, Mr. Deeds?"

Charles was shaking his head in disbelief. "That was my mother," he said. "And that was my childhood home."

They could all see that Mr. and Mrs. Ito were surprised by this revelation but Mrs. Ito carried on resolutely. "We found several things there," she said. "Some beautiful ceramics…of course…they…," she faltered, "they should be yours, shouldn't they Mr. Deeds? You must have them back."

Charles was quick to answer, "No, no, dear Mrs. Ito. They are yours. I had the chance to take anything I wanted years before, when my father died. I was happy to know that everything else would find a good home. And I couldn't be more pleased that they found a home with you." He smiled warmly at them. "I'm honoured to think that something from my childhood has a place in your home. It binds our stories even more closely together."

Mr. Ito spoke softly. "We will not forget these things that have brought us together, Mr. Deeds."

Loki, who had been sitting quietly, not an easy task for him, now jumped into the conversation. "And the box of books, Mrs. Ito?" he asked.

"Of course," she smiled. "Of course. While we were packing up the ceramics your mother asked if we'd be interested in any of the boxes of books. She wasn't selling them, just giving them away. We wanted to help her and we said we'd take two boxes. I looked at one and saw that they were classics—Dickens, Twain, Yeats, some paperbacks, some hardcovers. So I asked Mr. Ito to take that box and one other. I did not even look in the other box. We put everything into the car and took it back to our residence in Alfred. We didn't unpack anything as we were leaving for Japan soon. So everything travelled back with us and ended up in our home in Matsushima. My husband unpacked the ceramics. I forgot about the books."

"And you brought them here with you," said Loki.

"Yes," said Mrs. Ito. "I had always intended to sort through them, but by the time we moved here and settled in to build my husband a studio and find our way in this community, the house was filled with our children and their children and I just never did it. I thought it would be a project for retirement." She smiled at her husband who was nodding agreement.

"What made you finally sort through the things?" said Loki. "I know you haven't retired yet, Mr. Ito. I went to a showing of your most recent work last month."

Mr. Ito answered. "I haven't retired but the old family house is far too big for us now. One of our sons will be moving into the house with his family, so I'll still be able to use my workshop. We're moving to those lovely new apartments at the end of the village. We'll be able to go to Bean Cabin for Peter's pastries every day now."

"Oh no, we won't!" said Mrs. Ito. They all laughed and the moment was light.

Charles brought them back. "But…the box of books you dropped off here. Surely your grandson, the archaeologist, would have recognized Carter's book?" he said, puzzled.

"I didn't even open the box," said Mrs. Ito. "There's so much stuff to sort out and I thought I remembered it just being the classics. So I didn't even undo the packing tape that's been there since we first picked up the box in New York. The other box, the one with the classics, must still be at the house, waiting to be donated."

"Incredible!" said Loki, with enthusiasm.

"What a story," said Keeley.

Charles was lost in thought and they all looked at him. He spoke at last. "It must be the historian in me," he said, "but I can't help but think what an epic tale this is. It's like an ancient legend, where the affairs of man are directed by the gods. So many lives have been woven together to reach this point in the story. This is a tale of lost things, perhaps even lost souls. There's only one god I can think of who would do this; he's the guide on the journey between this life and the next, the guardian of the scale that weighs our hearts in judgment against the feather of truth, to see whether we are good or evil."

He spoke the name like an incantation. "Anubis."

CHAPTER TWELVE

Mr. Ito broke the spell. "Mr. Deeds," he said, quietly. "It seems certain to me that fate—perhaps, as you say, through the design of ancient gods—has brought us together. Will you come and have tea with us soon? We'd like you to meet our grandson. You two have so much in common."

Charles came back to the present day. "I'd be honoured to," he said.

Keeley began to think of practical details. "Mr. and Mrs. Ito," she said, "we must let Corporal Gagnon know about this as soon as possible. Would you like to meet him here? Or I could ask him to come to your house?"

"Please call him now," said Mrs. Ito. "We are relieved to find that we've done nothing wrong and we want to help the police as much as possible. I think…" she looked at her husband, "we would appreciate it if he could come to our house. This is a lot of excitement for us in one day and I know my husband will be wanting to get back to his studio."

"You know me well," said Mr. Ito, standing and taking her hand. He led her back through the front of the store with Charles at their side. Keeley and Loki could hear them making arrangements to meet for tea.

Charles saw them to the door and came back for his book bag, shaking his head in amazement at the Itos' revelations. "Let's get back to it, Loki." He turned to Keeley. "I think the officers are coming in the late afternoon for the stake-out."

"Yes," said Keeley, "they'll be meeting Sherine here at four o'clock and she'll take them upstairs. By five o'clock the other two officers will be positioned in the woods."

"And the trap will be set," said Charles, enthusiastically.

While Charles and Loki climbed the stairs to Forest Folios, Keeley phoned Luc. He wasn't happy about missing the initial conversation with the Itos but Keeley convinced him that it had been the right thing to do.

"I'll go and see them now," Luc said. "Then I'll come to the shop so you can let me know if they remembered to tell me everything they said to you."

At five o'clock Keeley sent Arwen, Scott and Sherine home to their university residence. Sherine was buzzing with excitement. The two plain-clothes RCMP officers had come in through the front of the store. Sherine had met them and given them a table lamp and a bag of clothes from the store to carry. She'd thought it all out. It would look as if customers had come to Past Life, been told about Folios, and then shown the way up there by one of the Past Life staff. Sherine had made a point of standing at the bottom of the stairs leading up to Folios, pointing to Loki's door and ushering them up. Then she quickly went back to Past Life.

Keeley smiled to herself as she locked up behind the students. Then she went upstairs to Folios. Loki was wrapping a book for his last customer of the day. Keeley could see no one else, but knew that the two police officers were in the kitchen with Charles. As soon as Loki locked the door Charles emerged, bringing his equipment and Carter's book with him. He positioned himself at a table near the window, in plain sight of the woods. It was dark outside and all the lights were on in Folios.

Keeley saw headlights in the back lane and glanced down to see the RCMP cruiser on its half-hour rounds. She knew she had to get out of there for the trap to be effective.

"Goodbye Charles," she said. "Take care of yourself." Impulsively, she hugged him. He was startled but responded with a warm hug. "Don't worry about me," he said. "I'm as safe as houses in here. Let's just hope he bites."

Loki saw her safely to her car. "Charles is staying with me tonight," he said. "He picked up his stuff from the hotel this morning. Makes sense when you think of the hours we're keeping."

Loki was going to Bean Cabin and Keeley was going home. Anyone watching Folios would believe that Charles was alone there, unprotected except for the police drive-by.

By eight o'clock Keeley's nerves were ragged. She knew she would have heard from Charles, Loki or even Luc if something had happened but she was beside herself with worry.

The phone rang at 8:15. It was Loki. "I've just come back to Folios," he said. "All safe and quiet here. No one tried anything. It's disappointing but we've still got tomorrow. I'm going to close the store down now, turn out the lights and let the officers come out of the kitchen and slip away."

"Oh I'm so relieved!" said Keeley. "It means he's still out there but I'm so glad that nothing happened."

"I didn't say nothing happened," said Loki. "Charles opened the back cover of the book and took out the papers hidden there. It's a letter, folded up. He insists on the three of us being together when he reads it. Can we come over now?"

"Of course!" said Keeley. "Come right over."

Her thoughts were spinning. A letter! Was this the answer they'd all been looking for, the reason for the break-in and the attack? How could an old letter possibly matter to anyone today, after being hidden in a book for nearly a hundred years?

When Charles and Loki arrived a few minutes later there was an urgency about them.

"Can I get you anything?" said Keeley. "You must be hungry Charles."

"All I can think of is the letter," said Charles. "Let's sit down and read it."

They all sat by the fire. Charles reached into his satchel and took out the book bag, with Carter's book wrapped again in the ancient linen. As he slowly drew the book out of the cloth they could see there was a small opening in the book's inside back cover.

"I put the letter back in, for now," said Charles. "It's been safe there for a century."

He took a pair of fine tweezers from his satchel and with infinite caution began to slide the letter out. "We'll be able to restore the cover completely," he explained.

The letter was in his hands. He opened it, leaned towards the light of the table lamp and began to read aloud.

> *I have buried her where no one will ever find her. Her soul is with Anubis now and he will find it wanting. I am not long behind her, but this story must be told for the sake of Teddy, my darling son, and those who come after him.*

Charles looked shocked.

"Oh my god," said Keeley.

Loki stayed calm. "Keep reading, Charles," he said. "We have to know."

Charles looked in horror at the paper in his hand. But he read on.

> *It began in April of 1924 when Howard Carter came to New York, riding the wind of the greatest archaeological discovery of all time— the tomb of Tut Ankh Amen. I had always been interested in ancient Egypt. In fact I'd collected a few artifacts at auctions, and was determined to take you, Teddy, to hear Carter*

speak at Carnegie Hall. It had been three years since your mother died, so you were six. If you are reading this...no...you cannot be reading this...but perhaps someone will read it to you.

A look of pain crossed Charles's face. "This is my grandfather, Joseph, writing," he said, apprehensively. But he carried on.

I decided that while we were in New York I'd try to make contact with my step-sister, Clara. We hadn't spoken since she'd left our childhood home. She'd written to me several times after your mother died, Teddy, asking to come and visit, but I had not replied. She was ten years older than I and had bullied me cruelly when we were young. I thought it was time to put all that behind us for your sake, Teddy. I sent a letter ahead, to the last address I had for her.

When we reached our hotel in New York she was already waiting for us there. She was dressed to the nines in high-heeled shoes, an expensive gown, bright lipstick and blonde hair I knew was not her natural colour. You were dazzled, just a little boy missing his mother, I think. I found myself wary, not wanting you to be near her, but she talked her way into having dinner with us and was so charming and kind that I thought my earlier impression was mistaken. I invited her to come with us to hear Howard Carter.

She sat through Carter's speech with rapt attention and I began to believe that she had truly changed. After the speech we went to buy Carter's book, this book. He autographed a card for me.

Charles picked up the book. "This book," he whispered. "This book."

"Go on Charles," Keeley encouraged. "Perhaps the first line is not what we think."

Charles read on.

While I was getting Carter's signature, awed to be in the presence of such a great man, Clara went to look at the artifacts he'd brought for the public to see. They were not the famous artifacts we've all come to know, but they were from the tomb—bits of pottery, little glass bottles and jars and pieces of cloth. There was an excited crowd around the table.

When we left the city to return home I invited Clara to come and visit us. I still didn't know much about her life but I wanted the chance to set our relationship on a new and better course. Within two weeks, she was at our door. I was surprised, but you had taken to her, Teddy, so we welcomed her into our home.

One evening she confided to me that she'd made a bad marriage to a man named Jack Mason who was a petty criminal and treated her cruelly. They had a son who was sixteen and a bully like his father. I sympathized and praised her courage for breaking away from them. I said that she was welcome to stay with us for as long as she needed to.

"I have never heard any of this," said Charles. "My father never spoke of an Aunt Clara or any other relative. He hardly remembered his own father."

He continued reading the letter.

I was busy with my medical practice and Clara was often left with you, Teddy. After she'd been with us about a month, tragedy struck us. When I came home from my office one day you were sick, Teddy. Your face was red and swollen. Clara claimed ignorance of anything that might have happened to you. I was horrified that perhaps I had brought something home to you from one of my patients. That night you became worse and worse. I thought I would lose you, Teddy, but you pulled through. Your fever broke and you went to sleep. But when you woke up in the morning, you were blind.

I was beside myself with grief for you. I neglected my practice to stay by your side.

Soon the word spread around the town that you'd been injured to the point of blindness. Suspicion fell on me and indeed I did blame myself for not taking care of you properly. Clara was indifferent. She was gone most of the time. I didn't care.

Then one day the police arrived. They were looking for Clara, her husband Jack and their son. The police had discovered that all three Masons were responsible for a string of violent crimes in the area. I explained that I knew nothing about it but they didn't believe me and told me they'd be back for me when they found Clara. Then…then Teddy—they told me I was an unfit father. They took you away and told me I'd never see you again.

Charles broke down in tears. The letter fell to the floor. "I can't bear it," he said. "It can't be true. My poor grandfather and father. How could I not have known about this?"

Keeley went to kneel beside him. She picked up the letter. "Charles," she said, her hand on his arm. "We'll help you get through this, whatever it is. Please finish the letter. Just get to the end and we'll decide what to do."

Charles pulled himself together. "Yes. I must, for my father's sake." He took the letter from Keeley and read on.

After they took you away I screamed and cried and raged and drank.

Then Clara came home. She knew what had happened. She laughed at the state I was in. She confessed everything to me. She had lied to me from the first moment we'd met up again in New York. She was elated at having succeeding in tricking me.

She told me that while you were in school she was meeting up with Jack Mason and their son, Granger. They were working together to commit several crimes, including armed robbery. They had been stealing from me too— she, Jack and her brute of a son. They'd taken your mother's jewellery, silver and glass, things I wouldn't miss.

I was beyond caring. You were gone. Life held nothing for me anymore. But then she told me one more thing, Teddy. She told me what she'd done to you. She boasted about it.

She told me that while I was getting Carter's signature she'd stolen a small cosmetic jar and a piece of linen from the artifacts table. In the chaos no one noticed.

"The linen…" said Keeley, "so it is from Tutankhamun's tomb?"

"Perhaps," said Charles, the professional in him giving him strength for a moment, "but I don't know yet." He looked down at the letter again and continued reading.

This is the part I don't want to write, but I must, for the sake of the future. Clara told me that the cosmetic jar she'd stolen still had traces of the original contents. She'd read about the substances from the tomb and knew some of them were poisonous and that some ancient poisons retained their potency over thousands of years. She was curious about the curse and decided to test the contents of the jar on you, Teddy. She put this noxious substance all over your face, my poor little boy. And it nearly killed you. It made you blind. And then I lost you forever. She did that. She did all that.

She had no goodness in her, Teddy, no remorse. She was pure evil. She said she was bored and it was all a game, to see what would happen—an experiment. And if I was too stupid to recognize it, that was my fault. She didn't care who knew anymore. She said Jack and Granger Mason were already heading west and she was going to join them. They were rich now. They would make new lives where no one knew them. She laughed. She laughed and mocked me and you, Teddy, until I caused her to stop.

Charles's voice broke. "I can't go on," he said. "I can't do it."

Keeley said, gently, "Loki, would you read the rest?" She took the letter from Charles's hands and gave it to Loki.

Loki's clear, calm voice took them back to a father's pain and desperation.

So I have buried her where no one will ever find her. And I will follow her soon, because there is nothing left for me in this life. I will leave this letter hidden in Carter's book, the ultimate irony, as that is where it all began. Before I go to the river I am going to give the book to my neighbour, whom I trust, with the instruction to keep it safe until you are of age, Teddy. Then it will be given to you. I don't know whether you will ever find this letter but I hope you will understand, my precious son, that I love you more than life itself. I deliver my soul to the Scales of Anubis.

CHAPTER THIRTEEN

Charles sat with his head in his hands. Keeley, who was still kneeling beside him, put her arms around him. It was too much for anyone to bear. Silence held them for a long time.

Then Loki said. "Charles, I'm going to call Luc Gagnon."

Charles nodded, saying nothing. He was completely withdrawn from them now, unreadable, in another time and place.

"I'll get us some tea while you do that," said Keeley.

From the kitchen she could hear Loki phoning Luc. When she brought the tea back Charles was still lost in his own world.

"Luc had news for us too," said Loki. "The RCMP officers stationed in the woods caught someone lurking around Folios after we'd left. When they asked him what he wanted, he took off. They caught him and they've taken him into custody. Luc is interviewing him right now."

Charles snapped back. "Then the trap worked," he said. "We have him! We'll find out what the hell is going on."

"Luc will be here in half an hour to see the letter and he'll tell us what he knows," said Loki.

"Then I suggest we have tea and sandwiches," said Keeley. "None of us has eaten and it's going to be a long night."

They agreed and Keeley went back to the kitchen to make some sandwiches. She could hear Charles and Loki talking in low tones but she was glad to be away from the white hot intensity of the letter and Charles's reaction to it.

They ate in silence. There was too much to say and no one could say it. It wasn't long until they heard Luc's car and Keeley went to the door. Luc was there in uniform. He had a woman with him, in plain clothes. Keeley recognized her and hesitated.

"This is Mrs. Maren Quayle," said Luc. "She's Crown Counsel."

Keeley shook her head at Luc. "What are you doing, Luc?" she said, angrily. She felt protective of Charles. "You've brought a Prosecutor? What for?"

"Keeley, Mrs. Quayle was present during the interview with the man we just picked up at Folios. So was Defense Counsel. It's procedure. I asked Mrs. Quayle to come with me. She's the one who'll have to determine whether there's anything to support a criminal charge here. Remember, we didn't catch the perp in a criminal act. He was just running away."

Keeley grudgingly stepped aside and ushered them in. "Forgive me, Mrs. Quayle. Our nerves are raw tonight and I was rude," she said.

Maren Quayle was in her early sixties. She'd lived in Cascade Canyon for many years, first as a partner in the law firm she shared with her husband and then, when he'd died suddenly fifteen years ago, as Crown Counsel. She wore a dark suit with a pink blouse and a string of pearls. Her salt and pepper hair was held away from her face by a couple of plain barrettes. She looked like someone's self-effacing grandmother. That notion shattered when she spoke.

"Understandable," she said, in a calm, direct voice. "I'm here to see that we follow the letter of the law. That law protects everyone, including you, Mrs. Carisbrooke."

When they reached the living room Keeley could see that Charles and Loki had heard the exchange at the front door. Loki was on his feet, looking wary. Charles was still sitting by the fire. He looked at Luc and the Prosecutor with empty eyes, his face blank and detached. He said nothing.

It was an awkward moment. Luc took the bull by the horns.

"Mrs. Quayle, I think you know Loki Andresson from the bookshop." Loki nodded at her, unsmiling. Luc went on. "And this is Charles Deeds. Mr. Deeds this is Maren Quayle, Provincial Crown Counsel."

Maren stepped towards Charles. He recoiled, almost imperceptibly, but she simply held out her hand. To refuse it would have been unthinkable for Charles and he rallied, stood up, shook her hand and met her eyes. They looked at each other for a long moment, sizing each other up, considering what they were up against.

Maren moved quickly away from Charles to shake Loki's hand.

"Sit down, please, everyone," said Keeley. She was feeling exhausted and mistrustful, completely overwhelmed by events.

They pulled chairs around the fire.

Luc launched into the subject at hand. "The letter, Mr. Deeds? Where is it? Can we see it?"

Keeley realized that the letter was nowhere to be seen. Loki had been reading it last, she thought. Where was it? Where was the book—and the linen cloth?

"No," said Charles coldly. "You can't. Not until you've told me what you discovered from the man you caught tonight. At this point you have no right to see the letter."

Luc bristled but Maren intervened. "You're absolutely right, Mr. Deeds, we don't. But I hope you'll see your way clear to showing us once we've told you what we discovered in the interview. Please continue Corporal Gagnon." It was clearly not a request.

Grudgingly, Luc began. "It happened when the officers concealed in the woods were just about to leave. You were all here and so was the book. It looked as if no one was coming for it. Then the officers noticed someone on the steps leading up to Folios. They moved closer and saw him try the door. He was pulling something out of his backpack when they challenged him. He ran down the stairs but they were already there. They brought him in."

"Who is he?" asked Loki. "Is he anyone you know? Did he tell you anything?"

"I'll get to that," said Luc, "but no, he's not known to us. It's more likely that he's known south of the border. He has a US passport. We contacted our counterparts and they're looking through their files."

"Another American connection," said Loki. Charles sent him a warning look and shook his head.

"What do you mean?" said Luc.

"I'll say this again, Corporal Gagnon," said Charles. "We will give you no more information until you tell us everything you know." Loki got it and kept quiet.

Luc showed his frustration but carried on. "We don't know that much," he said. "The guy told us he'd been hired over the phone and money had been e-transferred to him. He was told to get the book, by any means. He was the one who attacked Declan although he claimed it was in self-defense. That won't hold up," he said, quickly, as Keeley, Loki and Charles protested. "It was just chance and timing that led Keeley to ask Loki to put the book in the Folios safe that first night. If she'd waited until morning, the book would have been gone."

"Who is he?" Charles demanded. "Who's he working for? You must know that, at least."

Luc looked at Maren, who nodded.

"His name is Ryan Bricklow, according to his passport. I imagine our colleagues south of the border will tell us he's some kind of break and enter guy for rent. As for who he's working for, we don't know yet. But we traced the e-transfer and we know who paid him, well, we know the source but not the individual. The money came from Mason Conglomerate, in Oregon."

Keeley gasped. Charles stood up. "Mason, did you say? Mason Conglomerate?" His voice was deadly calm.

"Yes, in Portland, Oregon. You've probably heard of them, even on your side of the pond," said Luc. He looked around the group. "We all have. Known for lumber, mining—legendary robber barons once, with a questionable past. Their current business practices are still questionable, often predatory, skimming the surface of the law without actually breaking it, or maybe they're just good at not getting caught. They've been in the news a lot lately because their CEO, Sayer Mason, is running for Congress. We've seen his ads plastered all over the American TV channels, trying to sanitize the history of his family business and make himself a squeaky-clean candidate."

"But that's…" Keeley started. Charles interrupted her. "That's interesting," he said. "Perhaps we'll find out more when you hear back from your colleagues in Oregon." It was clear to Keeley that he didn't want to say anything about the Mason connection. She kept quiet.

Luc was impatient. "The letter, Mr. Deeds, will you show it to us now?"

Charles was quiet for a moment. "I will," he said slowly. "I will, but I wonder if you would allow me a few moments in private to read it over again first. I've only read it once and it's so emotionally charged, so full of tragedy for my family…" he trailed off.

Luc began to object but Maren jumped in. "That seems reasonable, Mr. Deeds. Will fifteen minutes be enough for you?"

Charles looked at her, relieved and thankful. "Yes, of course, thank you," he said. "Keeley, can I just go into the kitchen?"

"Of course," she said. "Help yourself to more tea while you're there. There's a pot on the counter."

Charles picked up his teacup and his satchel and went into the kitchen, closing the door behind him. They heard him refill his cup and help himself to milk from the fridge.

Taking advantage of his absence, Keeley asked, "Why are you really here Mrs. Quayle? Is Charles in trouble? Or any of us? I hope the Itos won't be dragged into this."

Maren was quick to reply. "No, of course not. The Itos have done nothing but be good citizens. I must admit to being cautious about Mr. Deeds. He's an unknown entity to us…"

Loki protested. "He isn't!" he said. "He's a friend of a close friend. He's been straightforward with us ever since he arrived, tried to help us, put himself at risk."

"All that's true," said Maren Quayle, "and it seems that coincidence brought him here to evaluate Howard Carter's book, but I've seen too many things in my career to believe in coincidence."

"The letter will make it all clear," said Keeley.

"Speaking of the letter," said Luc, "he's had enough time. I'm going to get him."

"I'll go," said Keeley, getting up quickly, remembering the impact the first reading of the letter had on Charles.

She opened the kitchen door.

Charles was gone.

So was Carter's book and so was the letter.

CHAPTER FOURTEEN

"Charles!" Keeley called out sharply. "Charles!" But she knew it was too late. The back door of the kitchen led to the back stairs down to the lane. The door was open. He was gone.

Luc was on his feet, moving fast, pulling out his radio. "Patrol, Code 10-30 E, we're looking for a man who just left…." Luc was running down the back stairs and into the lane.

Maren Quayle and Loki came in. Loki looked at Keeley in disbelief. "What happened?" he said. "Where is he?"

'He's gone," said Keeley. She turned to Maren. "I don't know where. Reading the letter was enormously stressful for him. He probably just wants to get away from all the questions and accusations."

Maren was unmoved. "There were no accusations, Mrs. Carisbrooke. A crime has been committed. One of your own staff was attacked. I'm sure you want to get to the bottom of this just as much as the police do."

The mention of Declan drained Keeley's anger. "Of course," she said. "I just feel so sorry for Charles. He's had a huge shock and we've come to think of him as a friend."

"Why don't we go back to the other room," said Maren. "And you can tell me as much as you remember of what was in the letter."

"Alright," said Keeley with resignation, walking into the living room with Maren.

But Loki intervened. "With the greatest respect, Mrs. Quayle, it's not ours to tell. Charles clearly didn't want to show you. I'm sure that's why he took off. Keeley, we need to get legal advice before we say anything else."

Keeley knew he was right and was grateful to him for thinking fast.

Maren was pragmatic. "Please do that as soon as possible," she said. "Withholding information can harm a criminal case."

"Right away," said Loki. "I'll call Tom Williams." He pulled out his phone and went back to the kitchen.

"Mrs. Quayle, can I get you some tea?" asked Keeley. "It's all been such a turmoil and I've forgotten my manners completely. Please forgive me. Some tea? A sandwich or a biscuit?"

"I'd love a cup of tea and a biscuit, please," said Maren. "And don't apologize. I'm used to seeing people at the most stressful times of their lives and I know not to judge them for that." She sat in one of the armchairs by the fire.

Keeley was back quickly with tea and a plate of biscuits.

Maren said, "I'm not trying to trip you up or get you to reveal anything until you get advice from Mr. Williams but is there anything at all you can tell me to help me get to grips with this? Why do you trust Mr. Deeds, for example?"

Keeley was quiet as she thought about the question.

"We only met him a few days ago," she said, "but he came to us through a mutual friend, Elizabeth Liang. Elizabeth is a costume designer in the movie industry. Loki and I have known her for years. We're all friends with Elizabeth—Loki and I, Rory and Declan. Have you been told that when I first unpacked Howard Carter's book it was wrapped in some kind of cloth?"

Maren nodded and Keeley continued. "We thought it might be very old, so we called Elizabeth to come and see it because she knows a lot about textiles. When she heard about it being wrapped around Carter's book she suggested Charles, whom she's known for years. He's a scholar, a professor, an archaeologist and an expert in ancient Egypt. Charles flew here from London immediately. We were surprised that he came so fast, but now we know he believes the book belongs to his family. And in the short time we've known him he's earned our trust."

Maren answered. "So leaving tonight in the way he did seems to be out of character? It looks as if something in the letter drove him to do that. Would you agree?"

Clever, thought Keeley. She answered carefully. "I don't know. I know he was terribly upset. Let's wait for Tom Williams and perhaps I'll be able to tell you more."

Maren nodded, satisfied that she wasn't going to get any more information.

"You probably don't remember me being in your shop," Maren said, making conversation, "but I know Declan well. I'm a classical music lover, a collector of recordings of *The Last Night of the Proms*, wherever in the world they are performed. Declan always keeps them for me, if any-thing comes into your store. He knows I love Elgar."

Keeley was surprised. "I haven't seen you there," she said. "But I'm often in the back while Rory and Declan and the students are in the front."

Then Maren dropped all formality. "I was so upset when I heard about Declan, the dear, sweet man," she said. "Please tell him I send him my best wishes for a good and fast recovery."

"I will," said Keeley, deciding in that moment to trust Maren Quayle.

Loki came back in. "Tom Williams is on his way," he said. "Luckily...not for him I guess," he said with a wry smile, "he was putting in some weekend time at the office and had just got home when I called. He advised us to wait until he gets here before we say anything." He looked anxiously at Keeley and Maren.

"It's OK, Loki," said Keeley. "Mrs. Quayle and I were just talking about Declan. She's one of his collectors."

Loki looked relieved and sat down to join them.

Luc came bursting in through the back door. "No sign of him!" he said, furious. "He's just vanished into thin air. How could he do that? He doesn't even know the area. He doesn't have a car or any of his luggage. Where's he going? You must have some idea!" he said heatedly to Keeley and Loki, who looked back at him resolutely.

"Tom Williams is on his way, Luc," said Loki. "Maybe we can say more then."

"What?" said Luc in disbelief. "Why do you need a lawyer?"

Keeley told him. "We know what's in the letter and it might be related to where Charles has gone, but it's not our letter and Charles obviously didn't want to give it to you. So we're getting advice."

Luc glowered, but Maren said, "They're within their rights, Corporal Gagnon. And we want whatever evidence we gather to be admissible, so we're going to do this by the book."

Luc sat down, still shaking his head in exasperation.

There was a knock on the front door and Keeley went to open it.

Thomas Williams was a third generation lawyer in the firm his grandfather had founded. His grandfather, Albert, had been one of the first Indigenous Canadians to graduate from the University of British Columbia Law School in the 1960s. Since then, Williams, Stephens, Williams had grown to be one of Vancouver's top firms, working on landmark cases, serving on several high profile First Nations committees and National Advisory Boards. Tom was in his mid-thirties and carrying on the family tradition of breaking barriers and being a champion for justice. He lived with his family in Cascade Canyon, a few minutes' drive from his office on the waterfront, which stood among gleaming glass towers, but most importantly to Tom, on his ancestral territory.

"Tom, good to see you. Come in," said Keeley. She knew how lucky they were to have him as a friend. He'd was always involved with big cases but never too busy to help his friends and his community.

"It's been too long, Keeley," he said. "You and Arwen must come and have dinner with us soon."

"We'd love that," she said. "Can I take your coat?" He was still dressed for work in a dark suit and white shirt. His tie had a subtle First Nations crest on it. Keeley knew it was Wolf, for his Clan.

Tom walked into the living room and acknowledged everyone. "Mrs. Quayle, Loki, Corporal Gagnon." Tom knew Luc well but this wasn't the time for informality.

"Please sit down Tom," said Keeley.

"Let's make this as fast as possible," said Luc. "We have a fugitive out there and time is passing."

Tom looked unruffled. "Tell me what this is about," he said.

Between them Keeley and Loki told the story, starting with finding Carter's book and ending with the letter. They were careful not to mention the contents or say anything about Charles's family history.

"Then I went to get him and he was gone," said Keeley.

"We need to know what's in that letter, Tom," said Luc. "And fast."

Tom considered. "I need to speak with Keeley and Loki alone," he said. "Then I'll decide what happens next."

Luc started to protest, but Tom silenced him. "Corporal, I know how important this is. I get it. We'll do this as quickly as possible. I suggest you and Mrs. Quayle either wait here or at the station. This is going to take at least half an hour, maybe more."

Luc knew that was the best he could get. "Mrs. Quayle, it's late," he said. "Why don't I take you home and come back here to see what Tom advises. We'll pick this up in the morning. We might have found him by then, you never know." He shrugged in resignation.

They said their goodbyes and Tom, Keeley and Loki went back to the chairs by the fire.

"Now," said Tom, "tell me what you remember of the contents of the letter."

They told him. "Mason," said Loki. "Jack Mason was the criminal married to Clara. The Masons did all those awful things to Charles's grandfather. Clara blinded his father. And we think Charles's grandfather killed Clara and then killed himself. At least that's what I got from it. Did you, Keeley?"

"Yes," said Keeley. "Mason. When Luc told us that they'd caught the guy who broke into Past Life and hurt Declan, he said they'd found out that he was in the employ of Mason Conglomerate in Oregon. That's what triggered Charles. I think that's where he's gone."

Tom sat up. "Mason Conglomerate? Sayer Mason? Not the best reputation in legal or environmental circles. We'll have to tell the police some of this," he said. "If Mr. Deeds goes to confront Sayer Mason he could be putting himself in a lot of danger. And there's obviously much more to this whole thing. Why would a guy like Sayer Mason send a petty thief to steal a book? You said even Mr. Deeds didn't know about the letter or the Mason connection until tonight. How could Sayer Mason know?"

Keeley and Loki couldn't answer that. But it was clear that's where Charles was going. They were so worried about him.

Luc was back soon, determined to get answers.

Tom spoke on their behalf. "Corporal Gagnon, Luc, I've advised Keeley and Loki that we should tell you a few things they remember about the letter. In my opinion they are the only things relevant to the investigation at this point." He looked at Keeley and Loki, who stayed quiet, relieved that he was taking the lead. "I'm going to paraphrase. You two jump in if I'm getting it wrong."

Luc took out his notebook.

"The letter was written about 100 years ago by Charles Deeds's grandfather Joseph, a widower, a medical doctor, who lived in New York State. In it, Joseph explains to his son Teddy, who is Charles Deeds's father, about how they were duped, robbed, injured and ruined by a man named Jack Mason, his wife Clara and his son, Granger."

At the mention of the name Mason, Luc stopped writing in surprise. He'd made the connection instantly. "Granger Mason the lumber baron? Sayer Mason's father? Mason Conglomerate!"

Tom nodded and carried on. "Teddy, Charles's father, who was then a little boy, was deliberately and permanently blinded by the Masons, with the result that he was taken away from Joseph and placed in a foster home. Joseph never saw him again. Joseph lost everything—his child, his professional medical practice, his reputation. We believe all that loss and grief drove him to take his own life." Tom gave a warning glance towards Keeley and Loki and they understood that no more should be said.

"Did Deeds know any of this when he came here?" asked Luc.

'Nothing," said Keeley. "It came as a complete shock to him. He'd never known how his grandfather died and his father never spoke about his childhood. Charles assumed he was blind from birth."

"What has this got to do with the book and the attack on Declan?" asked Luc, shaking his head. He was slowly starting to put things together and answered his own question. "The letter was in the book and someone wanted it. Sayer Mason wanted it, to stop it from getting out and ruining his run for political office. But how did he know about it?"

He got to his feet. "None of that matters right now. Deeds has gone after Sayer Mason hasn't he? He wants to get the guy who hurt his family. He's gone to Oregon."

"We don't know that for sure," said Tom. "We have no reason to believe that Charles Deeds is a violent man but there is reason to fear for his safety if he takes that course of action."

"He's got two hours' head start!" said Luc, making for the front door. "I'll alert the airport and the border authorities to watch for him. We have to find him and stop him."

"Corporal Gagnon," said Tom, reinforcing their professional relationship again. "Please keep us informed. I'm going to represent Charles Deeds if he wants me to, and Keeley and Loki need to know that their friend is safe."

"I'll keep you posted," said Luc, opening the door. He paused and turned back. "Thanks. I know you've all moved as fast as you could on this and I appreciate it." He left.

The fire sputtered and blazed as the draft from the closing door caught it and sent sparks flying.

Keeley was desperately worried. She hoped that Charles was safe out there, wherever he was going and whatever waited for him at the end of the journey.

CHAPTER FIFTEEN

Keeley was awake at dawn the next morning after a restless night. Too much had happened and she couldn't take it in. She made coffee in the kitchen and sat watching the first light of the sun paint the mountain peaks with gold. It was Sunday morning, even more quiet than usual in Cascade Canyon. A pair of ravens, aerial acrobats, swooped across the woods behind the house, calling to each other in their mysterious language.

She wondered how early she could call Loki. She needed the company of someone who knew all about this, someone who'd been there from the beginning. She thought, not for the first time, that it would have been nice to have Loki right there, to wake up with him…

Her phoned chimed a text. It was Loki. *U awake?* She smiled to herself. Sympatico, she thought.

Yes, she sent back. *Want to come over for coffee?*

Be right there.

She changed quickly into jeans and a fleece hoodie, Cascade Canyon's cold weather uniform. By the time she'd put another pot of coffee on, Loki was at the door. She hugged him, holding on. He held her tightly. She felt safe and reassured and with a sigh, released him.

"Look what I found," Loki said. He held up a brown paper bag. "I had some of Peter's pastries in the fridge at home. I bought extra because I know Charles likes them…" his voice trailed off.

"Have you heard anything?" asked Keeley.

"Nothing," said Loki. "I thought maybe he'd get in touch but he hasn't. I'm going to check in with Luc soon. Is it too early now, do you think?"

"Probably," said Keeley. "Let's have coffee and pastries and call him after that."

They sat together at the old pine kitchen table, in companionable silence.

Then Keeley said, "I'm so grateful for you Loki, for always being able to count on you. I couldn't have got through any of this without you."

He reached across the table and took her hand. "You know I'd do anything for you," he said. "I think, I hope, whenever you're ready we'll talk about being more than just good friends…that is… if you feel the same way. I don't want to pressure…"

She smiled and rescued him. "Let's talk about it soon, Loki. I woke up this morning wishing you were here."

That was all she needed to say. He beamed at her. "Let's go on a real date," he said, "as soon as we can, when all this is cleared up. And much as I love Yvonne and Peter's place I'd like to take you to that new restaurant on the mountain, where you can see forever and eat seafood fresh from the Inlet."

"I'd love that," said Keeley. "It's a date!"

They talked about mountain trails, fresh salmon, whether ravens could understand human words and how much snow Cascade Canyon would have that winter. They were in the middle of a debate about traditional or aluminum snowshoes when Keeley's phone rang. It was Luc.

"Morning Keeley," he said. "Here's what I have so far. Deeds managed to get to the airport last night and took the first flight to the US before our alerts went out. We know he flew to Portland. We're working with our counterparts there to find out what he did next. He must have taken a taxi or rented a car when he got there. At this point we don't know anything, but we'll find him."

"What about Mason?" asked Keeley. "Do the American authorities know that Charles might be headed there?"

"I've told them what they need to know, asked them to keep it low-key. I thought about what you said and I don't believe that there's a high risk to Mason from Deeds. Besides, Mason already has a security detail to rival the President of the United States."

"OK, thanks for letting me know, Luc," Keeley said.

"Will you tell Loki when you see him?" said Luc.

"I'll tell him now. He's here."

There was a short pause on the line before Luc said, "Ah, I see."

Keeley smiled to herself and decided not to set him straight. "Keep us posted, Luc," she said, about to disconnect.

"Wait, Keeley," said Luc. "You and Loki haven't heard from Deeds have you?"

"No, nothing," said Keeley. "We'd tell you, Luc."

He rang off and Keeley repeated the conversation to Loki, skipping Luc's comment about them being together that early in the morning.

"I really thought Charles would call us," said Loki, unhappily.

"Maybe he still will," said Keeley. "In the meantime I just want to keep busy. I think I'll go in now and do some sorting while the store's closed."

"I'll go with you," said Loki. "I can always use some quiet time at Folios."

Keeley was settled at her desk, sorting through some china teacups when all three of the students arrived. Safety in numbers, thought Keeley. Arwen came to give her a hug, with Scott and Sherine close behind.

"Is there any news, Mum?" Arwen asked. "Did the trap work?"

Keeley suddenly realized that they knew nothing about the events of the night before. She didn't know how much to tell them. She decided on as much of the truth as possible.

"The trap worked," she said. "The police caught someone trying to break into Folios last night after Charles and Loki left. They're working on finding out who is he and why he was doing it.'

"That's great!" said Sherine. "We all helped."

"Great news!" said Scott. "What did Charles find in the book?"

"He found a letter," Keeley said carefully, "written by his grandfather to his father. It was full of really sad things about his family history and he was terribly upset."

"Oh no! Where is he?" said Arwen. "Let's go and keep him company and cheer him up."

"Well…" Keeley was thinking fast. "He had to go on a sudden trip," she said. "Something in the letter prompted him to go and find out more. But I'm sure he'll be back soon."

They clamoured for information but Keeley turned them gently away. "I promise I'll tell you more as soon as I can," she said.

Scott and Sherine were satisfied with that and went off to Bean Cabin for coffee. Arwen lingered.

"Is everything alright, Mum?" she asked softly.

Keeley gave her a hug. "There's lots going on, Arwen and I wish I could tell you more but I can't right now. We're not in any danger though and the police are making good progress. Don't worry about me. I'm fine."

"And Loki is keeping an eye on you?" asked Arwen, smiling.

"He is," said Keeley. "How do you feel about that?"

"I'm happy for you, Mum," said Arwen, and with a quick hug she went to join the others at Bean Cabin.

By the end of the day they had still heard nothing from Charles. Luc got in touch with them in the late afternoon. "Nothing," he said. "Nothing here, nothing in Portland. He's vanished."

Keeley and Loki went to their separate homes, exhausted. They promised to meet at Bean Cabin for breakfast in the morning. For Keeley, it was another restless night. She dreamed of black water where an ancient crocodile waited for its prey.

☥

As soon as Bean Cabin opened on Monday morning, Keeley was at the door. Loki was right behind her. He looked as if he hadn't had much sleep either. Peter and Yvonne were taking the day off after a busy weekend. Their cheerful staff were serving comfort food and hot drinks to all who came in from the cold.

Keeley and Loki chose a table, ordered croissants and the waitress brought them hot chocolate.

The TV in the corner was on with the sound turned low. Friday's hockey game was being replayed and there was keen interest from several customers. A roar went up from the hockey fans as the home team scored a goal, all eyes turned to the TV and someone turned up the volume to get the replay.

Suddenly the announcer broke in.

> *This is breaking news. We're getting a report that Sayer Mason, the CEO of Mason Conglomerate, who is running for political office in Oregon, has been shot dead at his home in Hillside, Portland. Police are looking for a person of interest, believed to be visiting Portland from London, England by way of*

British Columbia. Again, Sayer Mason, controversial business leader and would-be politician, has been murdered.

CHAPTER SIXTEEN

Keeley and Loki looked at each other in disbelief. Keeley felt the world spin. Loki reached across the table to take both her hands as he watched her turn pale and close her eyes.

"Keeley," he said sharply. "Keeley, hold on, take a deep breath."

She could feel the warmth and strength flowing from his hands to hers and opened her eyes. "Oh god, Loki, do you think…?"

Loki cut in. "Let's not talk about it here. Too many people watching and listening. I'll get our order to go and we'll go back to Past Life. Drink some hot chocolate, Keeley. Hot and sweet. It'll help."

He got up to go to the counter and Keeley took his advice and took a sip of hot chocolate. Her thoughts were racing. Could Charles have done this? It was too much of a coincidence. Had they taken a murderer into their homes, into their confidence? She thought of Arwen and the others and found it hard to hold back tears.

Then Loki was back. "I have our order. Let's go Keeley."

He took her hand again and helped her up, then put his arm around her and walked her to the door, ignoring the wary glances that had been directed at them since the news report.

Back at Past Life, they found that Rory had opened the store and was serving several customers. He gave Keeley a worried look when she said hello to him. He knew her well and could read her distress, but she and Loki went quickly into the back room. They needed to talk it through with each other before talking to anyone else. The news would spread quickly around Cascade Canyon and Keeley wanted to be able to warn Rory, but first she needed to recover.

They sat close together at Keeley's desk, talking quietly so they wouldn't be overheard.

"Loki, do you think Charles did this?" she asked, with anguish. "Could we really have been so wrong about him?"

Loki didn't hesitate. "Absolutely not!" he said. "I know this looks bad for him, really bad, but I don't think he would ever do something like this. He seems to be a gentle person who was appalled by the violence that had happened to his family."

"But if he was in an altered state…" Keeley said.

"He had time to think about it," said Loki. "He had hours of travel and then a full day in Portland. I don't believe Charles has that in him."

There was a knock on the back door and Loki went to answer it.

Luc walked straight in. "You've heard," he said grimly, looking at their faces.

They both nodded.

"Have you found Charles?" asked Keeley. There was no point in beating around the bush. She knew what conclusions Luc and the Portland Police would draw from what had happened.

"No," Luc said. "I'm here to ask you again if you've heard from him. I don't need to tell you how serious this is. He's likely facing a criminal charge…"

Keeley and Loki interrupted, protesting strongly, but Luc carried on.

"If you've heard from him and haven't told me, that's obstruction of justice."

Keeley answered, angrily. "We've heard nothing, Luc. We said we would tell you if we did. Surely you trust us! We've had no contact at all since Charles walked out of my kitchen on Saturday night. You were there!"

Luc backed down. "I'm sorry, Keeley, just doing my job. Of course I trust you. Both of you."

Keeley calmed down. "Can you tell us whatever you know, Luc, please? We need to know."

Luc pulled up a chair and sat next to them. "Murder," he said, "that's public knowledge."

Keeley raised her finger to her lips. "Can we talk quietly, please Luc? Rory's in the front. He doesn't know yet and it will come as a shock."

"It's only a matter of time until he finds out," said Luc. "The whole town is talking about it."

As if on cue, Arwen and Sherine rushed in through the back door looking distraught. They'd left their classes when they heard the news. They saw Luc and reached for each other's hands. "It's true then?" asked Arwen. "Charles has… he is…I know he went …" she burst into tears and Keeley leapt up and put her arms around both girls.

Luc spoke quickly to reassure them. "We don't know anything yet," he said. "We haven't found Charles. All we know is that the timing is suspicious, but everyone keeps telling me in no uncertain terms that Charles couldn't do a thing like this." He paused and then said, "For now, I'm going to give him the benefit of the doubt."

The girls looked relieved and Keeley persuaded them to go back to classes. "There'll be lots of questions," she said, "because everyone who knew that Charles was in the village, after seeing him with us or reading his interview with the Courier, will recognize him from the description in the news reports. But don't say anything. Don't be drawn into any conversations. Just say we don't know any more than what's being said on the news. Tell Scott."

Arwen and Sherine left. Keeley knew they would be discreet.

"Luc," she said, "is there anything else? Where do you think Charles is? Do we know if he even saw Sayer Mason?"

"We know he did," said Luc. "Mason's housekeeper says Charles came to the door last night and she let him in to see Mason. She heard an argument but couldn't tell what was being said. Charles was still there when she went home."

"So we don't know when Charles left," said Loki.

"No," said Luc, "but late last night Mason's lawyer called the police to say that he'd found his client at the mansion. He'd been shot and killed."

"So Charles is a suspect?" asked Keeley.

"Well, we know he had motive and opportunity," said Luc. "We don't know if he had means, but guns are easy to come by in the States."

"Do you honestly see Charles Deeds as someone who would buy and use a gun?" said Keeley indignantly.

"People do strange things when they're angry or highly stressed," said Luc. "I've seen it happen a lot. And why hasn't he turned himself in if he's innocent? He must know the police are looking for him. It's on every news outlet in North America. Why hasn't he called you? He must know how worried you are."

Keeley had no answer for that.

But Loki did. "Something's happened to him," he said. "He's being held somewhere or he's hurt. Something's wrong. Otherwise he would have called us. I know it."

Keeley was startled. She hadn't thought about something happening to Charles but she knew Loki was right. He would have called. He would never leave them worrying like this, knowing what they were hearing on the news.

"We've thought of that," said Luc, quietly. "I've asked our counterparts in Oregon to check the hospitals and… any other places he might be if something is wrong. But so far there's no trace. He just seems to have disappeared."

There was nothing left to say. Luc left, assuring them that he would keep them informed. They promised again to do the same for him.

Loki left for Folios, reminding Keeley he was only one floor away if she needed him. She went to talk to Rory and in a quiet moment between customers she shared everything she knew. He and Declan had a right to know. He was shocked but he reassured her that he felt the same way she did. He believed in Charles's innocence.

After talking to Rory, Keeley sat by her desk for a long time, moving papers around without reading them. Realizing she was getting nowhere, she decided to join Rory in the front of the store. She spent some time with a lovely older woman who had come to find some teacups for a tea party she was hosting. They managed to find eight Paragon cups with fluted rims and patterns of spring flowers. Keeley wished she could go to the tea party—it sounded delightful. For a little while she forgot about all the drama of the day and enjoyed the peaceful delights of talking about teacups and scone recipes. She wrapped each cup and saucer carefully, added a pretty china serving plate as little gift and another satisfied customer left Past Life.

"Your phone is ringing, Keeley," said Rory. She hurried back to her office to get it. It was Luc.

"We found Charles," he said. "He's in a Portland hospital."

"In hospital?" said Keeley. "Is he OK, Luc? What happened?"

"Well, he's alive, but I don't know what happened. His car went off the road and down into a steep gulley. He has a head injury and he's been unconscious since they brought him in."

Keeley was alarmed. "Is he going to be alright, Luc? How serious is it?"

"He's being monitored. They say he'll live but it's too soon to know how serious the injury is."

Then a thought struck Keeley like a thunderbolt. "Luc, the book, the letter? Were they with him?"

"He had his wallet, his passport and his phone with him when he was found," said Luc. "But there's no sign of the book or the letter. They're gone."

CHAPTER SEVENTEEN

Keeley called Loki and he hurried downstairs. She told him what Luc had said. They sat in silence for a moment, then they both spoke at once.

"I think we should…" said Keeley.

"We have to go…" said Loki.

"Yes, we have to go to Charles, don't we? Who else does he have? And all this started with us finding his book. We have to help him."

"We do," said Loki. "I'll close Folios now. I can leave right away, but what about you, Keeley? You've got the students, the store…can you just pick up and leave?"

"I'm going to find a way," said Keeley. "Rory will be here. I'll ask him how he feels about handling the store on his own. And maybe one of the students has a light schedule this week and can help him out. We should only be gone two or three days. If it all works out we can leave in the morning."

"I'll make the travel arrangements," said Loki. "And one of us should let Luc know we're going. We should call Tom Williams, too."

"Could you do that, Loki?" said Keeley. "Tom might have advice and Luc's going to try to talk us out of it and I haven't got time. I will call Elizabeth though. She'll be desperately worried."

"Sure," said Loki. "I'll go back up to Folios and phone them now."

It was late in the day when Keeley finally locked the door of Past Life and headed home. Everything was in place. Rory was happy to handle the store and Scott would be able to help out every afternoon. Arwen was anxious about her mother going to Portland but her kind heart knew that Charles should have friends around him. Elizabeth offered to come with them but Keeley knew she was in the middle of a production, so she assured her they would call as soon as they got to Charles. Luc was unconvinced. He'd done everything he could to talk Loki and Keeley out of going. But when he couldn't change their minds he said he'd inform his Oregon counterparts to avoid problems when they went to see Charles and he made them promise to stay in contact with him. Tom was going to get in touch with a Portland lawyer, a colleague and friend of his, to act for Charles if he needed it.

A taxi was coming for Keeley at 7:30 in the morning. They would pick up Loki, go to the airport and be in the air by 10:30, landing in Portland before noon.

Keeley packed a small bag, had a cup of hot chocolate with Arwen, who was staying over, and finally fell into a restless sleep at about midnight. She didn't dream.

It was raining in Portland but coming from North Vancouver they were used to the rain. They took a taxi straight to the hospital. Luc had smoothed the way for them, so in spite of guarded looks and a few pointed questions, the police officer outside the door to Charles's room eventually let them in, making them leave all their bags and belongings outside with him.

Inside, the curtains were closed and the room was darkened. The only sound was the humming of machines and the shallow, ragged breathing of the man lying in the bed. He was still unconscious, his face pale, his head bandaged. He looked so weak and vulnerable that Keeley dropped into the chair beside the bed and took his hand in hers, holding back the tears. Loki, on the other side of the bed, laid his hand very gently on Charles's shoulder.

"We're here now, Charles," said Loki quietly. "Your friends are here."

There was no response. They stayed there in silence until a nurse came in. She seemed surprised to see them, ordinary people who were clearly friends of this high profile patient guarded by police. "One of you can stay," she said, "just one at a time, but I need to change his dressing now so give me ten minutes please."

They stepped outside. The officer was on alert, listening to their conversation.

"Keeley, why don't you stay," said Loki. "I'll go and check us into the hotel and come straight back and we can decide what to do next. Anything you want before I leave?"

"A coffee would be nice," she said. "Officer?" she turned to him. "Would you like a coffee?" He looked wary, then relaxed. They were clearly not a threat. "No thanks, ma'am, but it's good of you to ask." A small step in rapprochement.

By the time Loki came back with Keeley's coffee the nurse had finished in Charles's room and Keeley went back in. Nothing had changed. Charles looked as if he might never wake up. She took his hand again and sat there quietly. The nurse popped back in. "It might help if you talk to him," she said. "Some patients who are unconscious or in a coma can hear the conversation in the room."

She left and Keeley took a long look at Charles.

"Charles," she said softly. "Charles, I hope you can hear me. A lot of things have happened but the main thing to tell you is that you are safe now. We are here, Loki and I, and we are not going to leave you. You just have to come back to us and get better."

Charles stirred and sighed. Keeley felt his hand move in hers. "Charles!" she said, urgently. "Wake up, Charles, it's Keeley. You're safe."

His eyelids flickered and he opened his eyes. He looked around wildly, struggling to free his hand from hers but at last he was able to see her and recognize her. He calmed down.

"Keeley," he whispered. "What happened? Where am I?"

At this point the nurse, followed by a doctor and the police officer, burst into the room, alerted by the change in the machines monitoring Charles. Keeley held tightly to his hand.

"He just woke up," she said to the group. "He knows who I am."

The doctor pushed his way through to Charles's bedside, blocking the police officer, who had pulled out his phone. "Take that outside, please Officer," the doctor said. "Nothing is going to happen here until I say so."

Reluctantly, the officer went back outside. Keeley let go of Charles's hand. He was looking shocked, confused. "Mr. Deeds," said the doctor, "I'm Doctor Novak. You're in hospital in Portland, Oregon. You've been unconscious for two days. Can you tell me your full name and date of birth?"

Charles looked desperate. "What happened to me? How did I end up here? Keeley, what's going on?" He struggled to see her behind the doctor and the nurse and tried to sit up. She moved to his side again. "It's OK Charles," she said. "Just answer the doctor's questions."

Charles lay back against his pillow, breathing hard. Keeley could see the heart monitor registering his distress. "My name is Charles Edward Deeds. I was born in Watertown, New York, on May 14, 1960."

"Do you know what day it is, Mr. Deeds?" asked the doctor.

"It's…I think it's…Sunday? No…you said I'd been unconscious for two days. Is it Monday or Tuesday? What happened to me?" Charles's voice was getting stronger.

"We'll need the police officer here before we go into that," said the doctor. "But as far as I can tell there's no permanent damage. We'll have to run some tests to be absolutely sure but I think you'll make a full recovery."

"Oh thank goodness," said Keeley, smiling at last. But Charles still had questions.

"You must tell me what happened to me," he said. "The last thing I remember is going to Sayer Mason's house…"

"Stop, Charles!" Keeley commanded. She turned to the doctor. "If the police are going to interview him, does he need a lawyer? How do things work here?"

"Why should I need a lawyer?" asked Charles. "What do you mean?

"Doctor," Keeley repeated, "don't you think we need to tell him what's happened before the police come in?"

Doctor Novak nodded. "There are some things I can tell you, Mr. Deeds, but after that the police need to get a statement because a crime has been committed."

Charles nodded, puzzled.

The doctor continued. "Today is Tuesday. It's the afternoon. You were brought into Emergency on Sunday evening. Your vehicle had gone off the road and you'd been hit over the head."

Charles looked shocked. "Hit..? Who hit me?"

"We don't know, Mr. Deeds," the doctor said. "You were found beside your car, part way down an embankment in the Hillside neighbourhood. You were unconscious when you were brought in. We determined that your injuries were the result of someone hitting you over the head, not the vehicle accident. Portland police discovered that you had just travelled here from Vancouver, so Vancouver police were contacted." He looked at Keeley.

"Luc told us," Keeley said to Charles. "Loki's here too. We couldn't let you face this alone."

Charles was recovering from the shock of finding out he'd been attacked. They gave him time.

"Thank you, thank you both," he said, in soft voice, stricken with pain. "That's a lot to do for someone you've only met recently. It will be a relief to get out of here and go back with you to Cascade Canyon."

"No, Charles, I don't…" Keeley, began, but Dr. Novak cut in.

"Hold it," he said. "We must get the police back in here now."

Charles looked anxious and Keeley looked warily at the doctor as he went to the door and beckoned to the police officer outside to come into the room.

The officer shook his head. "Someone from our Detective Division is on her way," he said. "She'll be the one taking the statement from the suspect."

Charles heard the word and struggled to sit up again. "Suspect? What suspect? You know who did this to me?"

Keeley longed to tell him what had happened but a warning glance from the doctor kept her quiet. Suddenly Loki was at the door. He walked straight in, ignoring the officer. "Charles!" he said, smiling broadly. "Looking better than when I left. Good to see you awake. All good, doctor?"

"He's going to make a full recovery," Dr. Novak said to Loki. "We just need to run a few more tests and keep him here for a couple more days."

Loki nodded. "We'll stay until you get out of here Charles."

The door opened and a woman walked in. She was small, compact, wearing a no-nonsense dark suit, carrying a briefcase. The police officer hurried in behind her. "I told them they had to wait for you, Detective," he said. Keeley was surprised. This woman seemed young to have made it through the ranks so fast.

The woman spoke. "Who are you?" She frowned at Keeley and Loki. Then, to the doctor, accusingly, "What are they doing here? Has he said anything?"

Keeley started to speak but the doctor interrupted her. "We know what we're doing here, Detective," he said, coolly. "This isn't the first time we've handled situations like this. These people are his friends from Canada. He only just woke up and we've told him nothing. He has questions, naturally."

The woman climbed down from her brusque approach. "Sorry, doctor," she said. "This is such a high profile case. We can't put a foot wrong here."

She turned to Charles. "Mr. Deeds, I'm Detective Santos from the Portland Police Bureau. I'm here to interview you in connection with the murder of Sayer Mason."

Charles looked stunned, fell back and passed out.

CHAPTER EIGHTEEN

"Step back, all of you!" Doctor Novak ordered. They obeyed and he went to Charles, checking the monitors quickly. He took Charles's pulse, then turned him on his side and gently squeezed his shoulder. "Mr. Deeds," he said in a loud voice, "Mr. Deeds. Charles."

Charles stirred and opened his eyes. Loki put his arms around Keeley who buried her head in his shoulder.

Detective Santos stepped to the bedside and started again, "Mr. Deeds, I'm here to…"

"This will not happen," said Dr. Novak, cutting her off and turning to face her. "He's not strong enough yet."

She shook her head in frustration. "He's conscious. You said he'd make a full recovery. I'm going to talk to him now."

"You are not," the doctor said. "I'm going to run the tests I was going to conduct before you arrived. Mr. Deeds needs to rest. I suggest you come back first thing tomorrow morning." He turned back to Charles.

She was furious. "My officer will wait outside. I'll be back at eight o'clock tomorrow morning and I'll be interviewing him then or I'll be considering obstruction of justice." She marched out of the room with the officer on her heels.

The mood in the room came down a few notches. Dr. Novak turned to Keeley and Loki. "I need you to leave too," he said, "but you can come back in half an hour. It will do him good to see some friendly faces." He smiled reassuringly.

Charles, who was beginning to come back to consciousness, struggled to speak. Keeley leaned down to him and he whispered in her ear.

"Please tell me what happened," he said. "I don't understand what's going on."

"We'll be back in half an hour, Charles, just us, not the police," she said. "They'll be coming tomorrow but we'll have a chance to talk before they arrive. We'll tell you everything we know."

If Doctor Novak heard her comment, he ignored it. He was focused on the health of his patient.

Keeley and Loki went to the hospital cafeteria. It was getting late in the day and they'd missed several meals but they weren't hungry. They settled on hot chocolate and a shared muffin.

"Did he say anything to you before I came back?" asked Loki.

"No, he'd only just regained consciousness. But Loki, it was clearly a shock to him that Sayer Mason is dead. He obviously had nothing to do with it, but we know he saw Mason. I'm going to ask him about it when we see him. I don't care what the police say about talking to him. And let's call Tom Williams and get the name of his colleague here in Portland. I want Charles to have a lawyer present when he talks to the police tomorrow."

"I'll do that now," said Loki. "I'll be right back." He left the cafeteria so his conversation wouldn't be overheard.

Keeley pulled out her phone and called Arwen. She told her daughter that Charles had regained consciousness and was doing well but that he would be in hospital for a few days. She asked her to let Rory, Declan, Scott and Sherine know. Arwen encouraged her to stay in Portland as long as necessary. "We're fine here," she said. "Rory and Scott have everything in hand at Past Life. Mum…" she paused, "what about the murder?"

"I am absolutely sure he had nothing to do with it," said Keeley. "He was there and after that he was attacked. The truth will come out in the end and everyone will know that Charles is innocent."

"I believe in him, Mum," said Arwen. "I liked him from the first moment I met him."

Keeley trusted Arwen's instincts—and her own. "See you as soon as we can, love," she said. "I'll keep you posted."

"'Bye Mum," said Arwen, "I'm glad Loki's there with you. Love you."

Keeley's phone rang as soon as she'd ended her call with Arwen. It was Elizabeth. Keeley brought her up to date, reassured her as much as she could, and promised to tell Charles she'd called and was thinking about him.

Loki was back. "Tom is on it," he said. "He's been in touch with his colleague here in Portland who's agreed that his law firm will represent Charles if he needs it. That's a big relief."

They headed back to Charles's room. The officer outside the door nodded to them as they walked in. Doctor Novak was still there. "Don't stay long," he said. "He needs rest now. Just ten minutes and that's it for today." He left.

Charles looked much better. He was sitting up in bed, drinking water. They pulled up chairs on either side of his bed.

"I have so many questions," Charles said.

Loki answered. "Charles, we don't have much time, so I'm going to tell you what we know—all we know. It's not much. On Sunday, the day you were brought in, Sayer Mason was murdered in his home in Hillside. I don't know any of the details."

Charles interrupted, "But he was alive when I left! That much I remember."

"We believe you, Charles, of course we do," Loki continued. "But by the time you were found the RCMP had been in touch with Portland Police and they were looking for you—because of the book, the letter—because they thought you would want to confront Mason about what his family did to yours, maybe you'd want revenge."

"I did," said Charles, intensely. "I wanted him to pay for all the hurt his family had done to mine."

"Charles," warned Keeley. "Don't say anything else. A lawyer will be coming to see you, recommended by someone we know and trust in Cascade Canyon."

It was beginning to sink in. "A lawyer," said Charles, "I need a lawyer?"

Keeley took his hand.

Charles spoke again. "I want to tell you both, my friends who have come all this way, that on my father's life, I did not kill Sayer Mason. I did not hurt him. I wanted to but I did not. When I walked out of his house that night I didn't know what I was going to do, but all the rage had gone out of me. I was just desperately unhappy. I was thinking about my grandfather and all he went through. And my poor father, never being able to see the beautiful world he lived in and the faces of those he loved. I was just broken. The next thing I remember is waking up here with you talking to me, Keeley. The rest is a complete blank." Panic crept into his voice and Loki put his hand on his shoulder, to steady him. "It's alright Charles. We're going to get you through this. Everything will be OK. Just trust us to help you. You need to get some rest now. The police will be here to interview you in the morning. We'll be here with you and we'll have the lawyer. Rest now. It's going to be OK."

Charles nodded at them and closed his eyes. He looked so alone, so vulnerable. Keeley bent down and kissed his cheek.

"Arwen and Elizabeth send their love," she whispered, and quietly, they left the room.

They went back to the hotel. They were exhausted. Loki had booked two rooms for them and Keeley was grateful for time to be alone to pull herself together. She showered and fell into bed but not long afterwards she woke up shivering with fear. The stress of the last few days had finally found her. She got up in the dark, went to the adjoining door and knocked gently. Loki was there in an instant and drew her in to warmth, safety and the comfort of not being alone. In all the darkness, despair and devastation, they had finally found each other.

CHAPTER NINETEEN

Keeley woke up warm and happy—and remembered. Loki stirred beside her and they lay in each other's arms for a while, content. Then the alarm went off. Loki had set it when they'd first got back from the hospital to make sure they had time to get to Charles before the police arrived. It was six o'clock.

Keeley was getting dressed when her phone chimed with a text, sent to her and to Loki. It was from Tom Williams. *Reid Summers, from the Portland law firm Summers, Park, Leeson will meet you outside Charles's room at the hospital at 7:00. Good friend, good lawyer, good man.*

Keeley called to Loki through the open adjoining door and they left the hotel. They weren't far from the hospital and arrived there ten minutes ahead of Reid Summers. There was a different police officer outside Charles's door and they had to talk their way in again, but a nurse they recognized from the previous night came out of Charles's room and vouched for them.

They were delighted to see that Charles looked like a new man. He was sitting up in bed, with colour in his face and strength in his eyes. "Keeley, Loki, so good to see you!" he said, smiling. They smiled back at him and took their places in the chairs at his bedside. They were telling him about Reid Summers when the man walked in.

Summers was in his forties, a tall, striking Black man with startling green eyes which flashed fire. He took charge immediately and spoke directly to Charles. "I'm Reid Summers, Mr. Deeds. My colleague in Vancouver has told me about your situation and I've familiarized myself with what the police here know. But I'll need to hear it all from you."

He turned to Keeley and Loki. "Tom's told me about you. Good to meet you both. Time is short for us because the police will be here at eight o'clock to interview Mr. Deeds, so I'm sorry but I'm going to ask you to leave while I talk to my client." He turned back to Charles. "Assuming, that is, Mr. Deeds, that you'd like me to represent you?"

"Yes, yes I would. I'm grateful that you're here," said Charles.

Keeley and Loki found themselves on the way to the cafeteria again, more relieved than they had been in days. They discovered they were actually hungry and ordered a big breakfast.

Just before eight o'clock they went back up to Charles's room. It was chaos. Reid Summers stood in the doorway, blocking the entrance to the room. Detective Santos stood in front of him, almost a foot shorter but equally formidable. Several other people, including the police officer who'd been guarding the door, Dr. Novak, a nurse and another man stood beside them. Voices were raised.

"You will not come in and interview my client until we establish some ground rules," said Reid Summers, calmly.

"You have no authority to keep me out, Mr. Summers," said Detective Santos, furiously.

"I have every authority to defend my client, who, I remind you, has not been charged and is under no obligation to submit to questioning. I'll have him prepare a written statement." It was a threat and Santos recognized it as such.

"Then I'll charge him," she said.

Once again it fell to Doctor Novak to restore order.

"Step back, all of you. You too, Mr. Summers. I'm going in to check on my patient, to make sure he's up to this."

Reid Summers stepped aside but as Santos moved forward he blocked the doorway again.

"If the doctor says my client is well enough to talk to you I'll allow it," he said. "But you should know I've briefed him and he will not answer anything without my advice. So no tricks, just because this is a high profile case and you want an easy conviction."

Keeley and Loki looked at each other. They were in awe of Reid Summers. Loki even allowed himself a little smile. Glad he's on our side, thought Keeley.

"Agreed," said Santos. Her voice was quiet, cold and dangerous and Keeley suddenly had the feeling that she and Summers had faced each other down before.

Dr. Novak came back out. "He's ready," he said. "I'll give you thirty minutes."

They all moved towards the door.

"No," said the doctor. "You," he gestured at Santos. "You," he nodded at Summers. Then he turned to the other man, who had not been introduced. "Are you the stenographer?" he asked. "You'll be documenting everything that's said?"

The man nodded and lifted up his laptop to show them all.

"Then you can come in as well," said Dr. Novak. "Thirty minutes!"

Summers marched back in. Santos and the man she'd brought with her went in behind him. Keeley had a brief glimpse of Charles before the door closed. He was looking up at Reid Summers, calm and confident. She breathed a sigh of relief.

"Let's get coffee," said Loki. "We'll come back in thirty minutes."

Half an hour passed in a flash and they were outside Charles's door again. They saw Doctor Novak coming purposefully down the hall but there was no need for him to intervene. The door opened and Santos stepped through, followed by the stenographer. She threw an angry glance at Keeley and Loki and turned to the police officer at the door. "Come with me," she commanded. They walked away, leaving Keeley, Loki and Doctor Novak looking at each other in astonishment. Then Charles's door opened again and a beaming Reid Summers beckoned. "Come in, all of you. Good news."

He closed the door behind them as Keeley and Loki slipped into their accustomed seats at Charles's bedside.

Doctor Novak stood behind Keeley. Charles looked happy and relieved. He held out his hands to Keeley and Loki.

"Thank you for finding Mr. Summers for me," he said. "He's a miracle worker"

They all looked expectantly at Reid Summers.

"They have nothing to charge him with," said Reid. "No evidence. At this moment he's the victim, not the accused. They can place him at Sayer Mason's house on the evening of the murder because the housekeeper let him in. But Sayer Mason's lawyer, Hewitt Carradine—he's the one who found Mason and called the police—said when he was interviewed that Mason phoned him after Charles left. There's no evidence that Charles came back so he's no more a suspect than the housekeeper or a stranger. I put it to them that he could easily be a victim of the same person who shot Sayer Mason, someone who might think he saw something and ran him off the road during their getaway. They have nothing. He's free to leave as soon as he's well enough. He'll have to come back for the inquest or a trial, assuming they find the person who actually did this."

"Oh Charles, wonderful news!" said Keeley.

Loki leapt up and shook Reid's hand enthusiastically. "Thank you! Thank you so much!" he said as Reid clapped him on the back.

Doctor Novak moved quietly to Charles's bedside. "Mr. Deeds, it is good news, but you're not out of the woods yet. You've had a serious head injury and you still have no memory of how it happened. I'd like to keep you here for another day or two until I'm satisfied that you're well enough to leave. Especially if you're going back to Canada."

"Can he?" Keeley asked Reid. "Can he leave the country?"

"Yes, he's free to go," said Reid. "He's a material witness but they can't keep him here."

"Then you'll come home with us," said Keeley to Charles. "That's all there is to it. Arwen will be furious with me if I don't bring you back."

"You're coming back to Cascade Canyon," Loki said. "You'll stay with me until you're a hundred percent, Charles."

For the first time since the reading of the letter tears came to Charles's eyes. He gripped their hands. "It's almost too much," he said quietly, "to realize that I've found such good new friends at this time of my life."

"Mr. Summers," said Doctor Novak, "there's one more thing. It's possible, probable, that Mr. Deeds was attacked by someone who thinks he saw something or knows something. He's still in danger and the police have withdrawn their watch. I'm concerned for his safety."

"You're right Doctor," Reid said. "I came here today hoping for a positive outcome and as a precaution I've arranged for a private security firm to protect Mr. Deeds. I hope this will be alright with you. They'll sit quietly outside the door. I've used them before and I know they're the best, discreet and professional."

Doctor Novak thought for a moment. "Not something we usually do but in this case I know it's justified. I'll clear it with the hospital." He left, telling Charles he'd be back to check on him later in the day.

Reid Summers turned to go. "Time for me to leave as well," he said, "but I'm only a phone call away, Charles. Keep me posted on your plans. I'm going to call Tom Williams when I get back to the office so he can take over once you get back to Canada."

He shook hands with Keeley and Loki in turn. "Nice to meet you folks, even in these circumstances. Bring Tom with you next time you come and we'll all go to Deschutes Brewery and put the world right."

After he left Keeley and Loki turned back to Charles, who was looking tired.

"Charles, I have to ask," said Keeley, "do you know what happened to the letter and the book? Were they stolen when you were attacked?"

"They're safe," said Charles. "They're still in Cascade Canyon. I took photos of them with my cellphone and that's what I showed Sayer Mason. There's so much more to tell you but I just need to rest now. Will you come back later and I'll tell you everything about my meeting with Mason?"

"Of course," said Keeley. "We'll stay here in Portland until you're discharged then we'll all travel home together. Portland is a great town and they have some of the best bookshops on the West Coast." She exchanged a long, happy look with Loki.

"Ah," said Charles, smiling. "I see."

They laughed together and Charles settled back for a rest. As Keeley and Loki left, the man sitting in a chair outside the door reading a book looked up at them. He was wearing a navy suit with a gold logo on the blazer. After a long, careful scrutiny he nodded at them and went back to his reading. Charles's protection was in place.

CHAPTER TWENTY

Keeley and Loki visited Charles the next day, in the afternoon. He was much stronger and told them that Doctor Novak thought he might be well enough to leave on the following day. They celebrated with milkshakes acquired by Loki in the hospital cafeteria.

They avoided all talk of the murder and Charles's attack and instead Keeley and Loki told Charles about their morning. They'd spent hours in Powell's, the legendary bookstore. Loki raved that he thought he could find any book he wanted there, no matter how rare and obscure. Charles was determined to go there on his next trip to Portland. They'd picked up a couple of books for him, one on west coast flora and fauna and one on hiking trails of the Pacific Northwest. Loki pointed out a few trails near Cascade Canyon.

"We're going on this one as soon as you're well enough, Charles," said Loki, "and we'll look for some of those rainforest plants."

Charles laughed. "You're doing a fine job of convincing me how great it is to live in Cascade Canyon," he said. They looked at him, surprised.

"I've been seriously thinking about it," he said. "My term at University College London is finished and I've been travelling around consulting, as you know, but I can be based anywhere to do that. It seems to me that life has given me, a solitary man, a most wonderful and remarkable gift—a community of friends, something I've never really experienced before. Oh, I certainly had compatible colleagues and the occasional close relationship but I always held back and of course, I ended up alone. I've been given a second chance and I mean to embrace it as fully as possible."

"Charles, that's wonderful news," said Keeley. "I've already been grieving a bit that we would eventually have to say goodbye to you. Cascade Canyon will welcome you with open arms."

"It's a perfect fit!" said Loki. "And of course there are universities and museums all over BC's south coast who would love to benefit from your expertise."

They talked for a while about plans and possibilities and then Charles said, "I promised to tell you about the book and the letter."

They looked at him with concern, hoping it wouldn't bring back too much pain.

"When I left your house, Keeley," Charles said, "I had just one thought in my mind, to get to Mason and confront him with all the evil his family had done to mine. I went out the back way, as you know, and ran down the lane with the book, the letter and the linen cloth in my satchel, but I knew I couldn't risk taking them to Portland with me.

I stopped and photographed them and slipped the letter back inside the cover of the book. Then I kept running.

"As I ran past the Itos' house I could see Mr. Ito in his workshop. I took a chance and went in. I only had a moment. I asked him to do me a great favour and keep the book until I came for it again. Mr. Ito asked no questions. I didn't tell him about the letter as I didn't want to compromise him. He took the book and held it for a moment, without opening it. I gave him the linen cloth and he wrapped the book very carefully. Then he went over to one of his magnificent glazed pots. He lifted the lid, placed the book gently inside and replaced the lid. In the middle of all the stress and hurt, that simple thing brought me peace. 'Mr. Deeds,' he said. 'It is my honour to be the keeper of this book again until the moment you ask for it back.'"

"So the book's story adds another chapter," said Loki, thoughtfully.

"I haven't told anyone except Reid Summers. I want to protect the Itos and keep the book safe until I get back to Canada."

"The secret's safe with us," said Keeley. They chatted until the nurse came in to give Charles his medication and then they left, with a final, excited, "See you tomorrow!"

It was still early and they decided to take a walk in Portland's South Waterfront Park beside the Willamette river, through the winding greenways. It was a clear, bright day and they could see the volcanoes guarding the eastern horizon, cones and craters gleaming under caps of snow, living landmarks on the Pacific Ring of Fire. Being surrounded by big mountains felt like home.

There were many similarities between Portland and Vancouver but Portland has its own cool cachet, an easy mix of old and new. They both knew Portland well and decided to have dinner at Mother's Bistro and Bar, not far from the waterfront. Over a hearty meal of Mom's meatloaf and gravy they talked over the happenings of the day.

"You didn't tell him about the other book you bought at Powell's," said Keeley.

"I just thought it would remind him of everything," said Loki.

He reached into his bag and pulled out a copy of *The Tomb of Tut Ankh Amen.* "Not a first edition like Charles's but an early one," he said. "I had to have it."

Keeley reached for it and he handed it over.

"I really didn't have a chance to look at Charles's copy," she said. She opened it and found the photo of Lord Carnarvon facing the title page. "So he was already dead when this book came out," she said. "Part of the curse."

Loki looked at the photo. "Poor man," he said. "He died in Cairo from an infected mosquito bite, but look here," he turned the page and pulled out a piece of paper. "This clipping was tucked inside the book. It's from New York World magazine in March 1923. It's a letter about the curse from the novelist Marie Corelli. She was very popular then, a celebrity.

He read, "'*I cannot but think some risks are run by breaking into the last rest of a king in Egypt whose tomb is specially and solemnly guarded, and robbing him of his possessions. According to a rare book I possess … (an ancient Arabic text), the most dire punishment follows any rash intruder into a sealed tomb. The book . . . names secret poisons enclosed in boxes in such wise that those who touch them shall not know how they come to suffer. That is why I ask, was it a mosquito bite that has so seriously infected Lord Carnarvon?"*

"Poisons?" said Keeley, startled. "That seems to confirm the part in Charles's letter about Clara using the poison from a jar from Tutankhamun's tomb."

"It does," said Loki. "And there are some hand-written notes at the bottom of the clipping. *'No one knows why Marie Corelli sent this. She died the following year without ever revealing her reasons.'*"

Keeley was quiet. "Seems to me like the curse is still a threat," she said at last. "Look how it's hurt generations of Charles's family."

"I think it just proves that modern humans are every bit as hungry for wealth and power as the ancient Egyptians," said Loki.

They shared a spectacular crème brûlée and caught the bus back to their hotel. Although they left the door open between their two rooms, there was no need. It was unspoken between them that they would only need one.

By the time they reached the hospital the following afternoon, Charles was ready to go. He was sitting on the bed, still in his hospital gown, looking expectantly at the door. He'd asked them to buy him some clothes, since the ones he came in with were damaged beyond repair. He hadn't brought anything with him from Cascade Canyon except his wallet, passport and phone. Reid Summers had come to see him and given him assurances that he would be there to advise him again if it was ever necessary.

Keeley and Loki had bought Charles some casual clothes, a good coat and a small leather duffle bag. Charles was about Loki's size, although not quite as tall. While Charles changed, Keeley and Loki went out to the hallway with Doctor Novak, who gave them some final advice about what to watch for as Charles recovered from the head injury. They promised to take Charles to the doctor in Cascade Canyon to support his full recovery.

"It all fits!" said Charles, emerging from his room. He was dressed, looking tired, but smiling. He shook Doctor Novak's hand. "Thank you Doctor," he said, "not just for treating me but for keeping the angry hordes away."

Doctor Novak laughed. "Good luck, Mr. Deeds," he said. "I hope that if we meet again it will be under very different circumstances."

Loki held out his arm and Charles took it, grateful for the support. They had a taxi waiting to take them to Portland International Airport where Keeley had booked them onto an early flight out.

As soon as they were in the air, looking down on the chain of volcanoes strung out along the Pacific Northwest, Charles relaxed and fell asleep. They woke him on the descent into Vancouver International and within an hour a taxi was driving them up the main road to Cascade Canyon. It was early evening and alpenglow painted the high peaks. The trees were changing colour and turned their bright autumn leaves to catch the last light of the sun. It was breathtaking, as always. Keeley and Loki never took it for granted.

"Home," Keeley whispered.

"Yes," said Charles. "Home."

As they pulled up outside Keeley's house the front door `burst open and a large group of people rushed out towards them—Arwen, Scott, Sherine, Declan, Rory, Elizabeth, Tom Williams and Luc Gagnon.

Loki helped Charles out of the taxi and smilingly admonished all of them. "Back, all of you! Let the man come inside and rest."

Arwen, Elizabeth and Sherine came to give Charles gentle hugs. Keeley could see how it affected him. He'd had a lot to deal with and his emotions were close to the surface.

They all went up the steps and back inside where an enormous buffet was set out on the dining room table. Charles sank into a chair. Declan, completely recovered, pulled up a chair beside him. Rory brought him a cup of tea. Tom Williams came over to shake Charles's hand, leaned down and spoke quietly in his ear, then stepped back.

"Corporal Gagnon," Tom said. They all knew it was formal when he used Luc's title. "I'm leaving now and I advise you to do the same."

Luc nodded. "Mr. Deeds," he said, "there are still questions to be answered but I just want to say that we're all relieved you're OK. And just in case there's still any danger to you…" Arwen gasped. Luc went on. "…we'll be patrolling Loki's place until all this settles down."

Charles nodded, suddenly silent and guarded.

Tom and Luc left together.

"Charles, you must be exhausted," said Declan in his soft Irish lilt. "We wanted to welcome you home but just say the word and we'll all clear out."

Charles turned to him and relaxed. "Declan, you can't know what all this means to me. I'm so grateful to all of you. Please stay." He turned back to the room. "I'd love to have some dinner with you. It will be my first 'real' food in days!"

They ate together, laughed together, Declan put some music on, wine glasses were raised. And one by one, each person in the room came to sit next to Charles and speak to him quietly, to let him know they were glad he was home safely, until Arwen, who'd taken up her post on the floor at his feet, glanced up and noticed how tired he looked and declared the evening over.

Declan and Rory drove Loki and Charles home to Loki's house. Elizabeth went back to her downtown apartment. The students all went off together after helping to clear up. Keeley collapsed into her chair by the fire and gazed into the flames.

Since the moment Charles had come home no one had mentioned old books or letters, Egyptian kings, family tragedies and above all, murder. But they all still hovered like ghosts in the shadows.

CHAPTER
TWENTY-ONE

Luc insisted on a formal meeting with Charles the day after his return from Portland. They met at Loki's house after Loki had left for work. Charles asked Tom Williams to be there.

"I'm sorry for leaving the way I did, Corporal Gagnon," said Charles. "I can only say, in my defense, that I was beside myself with grief and was not thinking straight."

"You're a central figure in several criminal investigations," said Luc, to which Tom objected.

"At this moment, Corporal Gagnon, my client is a victim and nothing more. He may have useful information or he may not, but please be careful not to cast him as a criminal."

Charles stayed silent and Luc tried again.

"Can you tell us anything, Mr. Deeds, that might help us and our counterparts in Portland with this case? What is your relationship with Sayer Mason? Can you show me the letter? Is it still in Cascade Canyon?"

Charles looked at Tom, who nodded, and Charles reached for his laptop.

"I can honestly tell you, Corporal Gagnon, that I do not have the book and the letter in my possession at this time. But they are safe. Mr. Williams knows where they are and has assured me that I don't have to produce the letter unless the court requests it."

Luc started to protest but Charles continued. "I do have a copy of the letter. I'm sure you know by now from your American colleagues that I have photographs of the letter on my phone. I have them here and I'll print them out for you if Mr. Williams agrees."

"I don't see why not," said Tom. "But I insist, because of the deeply personal and private nature of the contents of the letter, that it be kept absolutely confidential and seen only by yourself at this point, Corporal Gagnon."

Luc nodded and looked eagerly at the laptop. Charles typed and in the corner of the room Loki's printer sprang to life. Tom Williams walked over to it, scrutinized the papers and gave them to Charles, who glanced at them with pain flashing across his eyes and handed them to Luc.

"Just give me a moment," Luc said.

He read the letter, his face registering surprise and sympathy, which he fought to control. When he'd finished he looked at Charles with understanding. He dropped all pretense of authority and spoke to Charles as an equal.

"I'm so sorry, Mr. Deeds, what a tragedy. You can be sure we'll do everything we can to solve this. You have my word."

Charles looked at him for a long time without speaking.

"Corporal Gagnon," he said at last. "I know you've just been doing your job. As one who hopes to become a permanent part of this community I'm grateful for it."

Luc looked relieved. He stood up and took his leave, carefully putting the copy of the letter in his zippered jacket pocket.

"Well Charles," said Tom. "The good news is that you'll be staying in Cascade Canyon. The bad news is we're no closer to finding out who killed Mason and who attacked you. Don't let your guard down."

About a week after his return to Cascade Canyon Charles asked Loki to go with him to see Mr. Ito. So on a cold morning, Loki and Charles walked down the main road past Bean Cabin, where Peter and Yvonne came running outside to greet them and Peter insisted that they stop by for coffee and 'cream horns on the house' on their return walk.

Kaito Ito's studio was at the edge of town. Charles had phoned ahead and Kaito was there, waiting at the studio door. He ushered them inside and bowed deeply. They bowed in return.

"Mr. Deeds," said Kaito softly, "It is so good to see you and know you are well."

Loki looked curiously around the studio where dozens of beautiful pots stood at various stages, some newly thrown, some glazed and glowing. He wondered which one held Carter's book and the letter, but knew he could not ask. Discreetly, he wandered to the far end of the workshop near the kilns, to give Charles and Kaito some privacy. He glanced back to see them deep in conversation. He saw Kaito nod and offer another deep bow to Charles. Charles returned it and held it, in a mark of respect for Kaito.

"Loki," called Charles, "Mrs. Ito has invited us for tea."

Loki was delighted. He'd had tea at the Itos' before and it promised to be made up of delicious Japanese sweet treats, refreshing green tea and stimulating conversation on topics from pots and politics to plants and poetry.

Kaito locked the studio door as they left. No clue was given about the pot containing the book and the letter and no mention was made of it over tea.

Charles recovered well. It was quiet and secure at Loki's and at first he spent his days reading books Loki brought him from Folios and listening to music Declan chose for him.

They heard nothing more from Portland. The police there were still working on the Mason murder and looking into the attack on Charles but according to Reid Summers, who kept in touch with Tom Williams, no progress had been made. Reid had attended Sayer Mason's funeral. He told Tom, who passed it on to Charles, that after the funeral Sayer's son Ryker had declared his intention to take over his father's run for public office. Charles had pointedly avoided listening to, reading or watching any news items about the Masons. He knew there was a chance it might jog his memory, which was still blank, but it was still too raw and he couldn't risk more trauma.

When he felt better, Charles walked through town every morning to Past Life and Folios, stopping at Bean Cabin for coffee. He allowed himself to have cream horns only on weekends, joking with Peter that until he was back at full strength he had to work hard to stay fit. After Bean Cabin Charles went to Past Life to visit whoever was there and was always greeted with warmth and high spirits. Then he went upstairs to Folios and worked with Loki to sort, acquire and assess books and help him send them out to collectors.

Each afternoon he went back to Loki's. He'd taken on some work editing a history book being written by a professor at the University of British Columbia—work he enjoyed and could do from home. Evenings were often spent with Declan and Rory or Keeley and Loki and the students. Sometimes Loki stayed at Keeley's. Charles was used to being alone. If he was afraid or anxious, he never showed it or spoke of it and life settled into an easy routine as the weeks passed.

November turned to December and Loki declared to Charles that it was time for them to hike in the mountains.

They geared up. Loki had offered to share some of his gear with Charles but Charles was already thinking of his future in Cascade Canyon and bought his own gear under Loki's watchful eye. Charles had hiked all over the world, but never in mountains as high as Vancouver's North Shore, which brought their own unique challenges. Being so close to the urban centre, people often underestimated the dangerous wilderness at their doorstep. North Shore Rescue was one of the busiest Search and Rescue organizations in North America. So Loki equipped Charles with all the essential winter survival gear, even though they were only going on a day hike.

They set out very early on a cold Saturday morning, with frost sparkling on the cedar branches and Christmas lights turning Cascade Canyon into a storybook village. There was snow on the Lions, the North Shore's highest twin peaks, but not on the lower trails and the cold air made the views sharp and clear.

The trailhead was near the end of the main road through Cascade Canyon. The village was still asleep when they set out but there were lights on in Bean Cabin. They joked to each other that Peter was probably making cream horns.

It didn't take long before they'd left all trace of human development behind. In the dense rainforest, Douglas fir, western red cedar, hemlock, and spruce battled each other for a place in the rising sun. Ferns, mosses, lichens, berry bushes, and salal bordered the trail, which was soft underfoot, carpeted with needles from the conifers.

At first, the trail travelled beside a small, sparkling stream. Ice was beginning to form at its edges but as the trail began to climb they left the stream behind. It was quiet, with only the occasional sounds of their footsteps and the creak of wind and frost in the tree branches. They stopped talking, enjoying the gift of peace the forest offered. They hiked on for about twenty minutes in silence, climbing steadily, when Loki, who was ahead of Charles, suddenly stopped short and held up his hand in the closed-fisted sign Charles recognized as *stop now!* Charles froze in place. Slowly Loki turned back to him and said, "Bear. Move to the side of the trail on your right so he has a clear path past us. Let's talk so he knows where we are and isn't surprised. I heard him over to the left."

Charles recovered. "I thought bears hibernated at this time of year," he said in a loud voice.

"Lots of bears who live near the city don't hibernate anymore," said Loki, as they both stepped carefully into the bushes at the right side of the trail. "I can't hear him now but he can hear us and he's deciding what to do. Bears don't want a confrontation with humans any more than we want one with them. We just have to give him the space to get away. Then we'll…"

Gunshots echoed through the air and sent them both diving to the ground. They looked at each other in shock and horror and another shot rang out, shattering the small branches of a nearby tree. "Is someone shooting at the bear?" Charles whispered to Loki.

Loki grabbed Charles's arm so he wouldn't stand up. "No." Loki was whispering now, fear edging his voice. "I don't think there is a bear. I think they're shooting at us. We need to move." He pulled Charles further back and they began to crawl through the thick bushes and ferns. After a few minutes Loki stood up and indicated to Charles that he should do the same. Then with Loki leading, they doubled back in a wide circle, moving fast. When they reached a small elevation Loki stopped. "We'll hide here," he whispered. "If he comes after us we'll be able to see him from up here." He pulled out his phone and called 9-1-1, urgently whispering information to the dispatcher.

They hid behind a huge fallen tree. Covered by tall ferns, they flattened on the cold ground. Loki kept watch. They could hear someone crashing through the under-brush but Loki was a skilled outdoorsman and had chosen the path of their retreat carefully. Half an hour passed. At first they could hear two voices calling to each other, searching for them, but no one came near their hiding place. People got lost in this forest simply by stepping off the trail. Loki hoped their luck would hold.

Suddenly, in the sky above their heads, the throb of helicopter blades thrashed through the silence. Charles and Loki looked up and right above them the RCMP helicopter swept across the tree tops. Loki took a chance and stood up, his bright orange jacket visible from the sky. Charles stood up beside him. The helicopter swung back and hovered above them and Loki's phone pinged. A text from Luc Gagnon. *We see you and we see them. Stay where you. Get back down on the ground. A search group is on the trail and will come to you.* Loki showed the text to Charles and they both sank back down to the ground in relief.

Loki pulled out his thermos and snack pack and told Charles to do the same. "We need to eat and drink," Loki said. "We're cold and we're probably in shock. Luc will take care of things. We'll just wait for them to find us."

Charles found his voice at last. "It's me again, isn't it? They're still after me. I'm so sorry to have dragged you into this Loki. I thought after all this time that it was safe." Worry etched his face.

"We've been through all this before," said Loki. "You're a victim here. Luc will catch the bad guys, Charles."

Charles nodded and poured himself a hot chocolate, trying to keep his hands steady.

Within a few minutes a team of six people arrived, calling out to them as they came, assuring them that they were there to help, not hurt. Fortunately Loki and Charles had not gone far off the trail and it was easy to reach them. As the team swung into view below the small rise where they were hiding Loki recognized the bright jackets and helmets of the volunteers from North Shore Rescue, NSR to the locals. He knew they could mobilize very fast and wasn't surprised that Luc had called them in.

They were friendly, professional and skilled. After checking Charles and Loki for injuries and making sure they were strong enough to walk, they escorted them back down to the trail and led them back to town. They could hear the NSR team leader talking on his radio to the helicopter, which made frequent passes overhead as they walked. They all arrived at the playing fields at the edge of Cascade Canyon at the same time, early in the afternoon. The whole event had only taken a few hours to unfold.

The helicopter landed, Luc jumped out and the helicopter returned to the air. Luc had a quick conversation with the NSR team leader and then came straight to Charles and Loki.

"Did you get them?" asked Loki.

"Not yet," said Luc, "but we know which direction they took. They can't go far. We'll get them." He looked at Charles. "I promise we'll get them. No one gets to come into our mountains and shoot at our people," he added angrily. "I'll need a full statement."

Charles swayed on his feet and both Luc and Loki reached out to steady him. "Let's go to Bean Cabin," said Luc, in a soothing voice, "find a quiet corner and you can tell me what happened in your own time over a cup of coffee and a cream horn."

This calm approach was so unlike Luc that they looked at him in amazement. "Victim assistance training," said Luc proudly.

By the time they reached Bean Cabin a table had been set aside for them in the corner, away from curious listeners. Peter had already put a large plate of cream horns on the table and as they walked in he brought over three steaming mugs of coffee. Then, with a slap on the shoulders for Luc, Peter retreated behind the counter to make sure they weren't interrupted.

They had just taken their first sips of coffee when Luc's radio barked and he reached for it. "OK," he said. "OK good. I'll be back at the station within an hour."

He put the radio back in his belt and turned to Charles and Loki.

"Got them," he said.

CHAPTER
TWENTY-TWO

Word travelled fast. Keeley and all the students were waiting for them after they left Bean Cabin and arrived at Past Life. After hugs all round they went inside and told their story again, ending with the news that the RCMP had caught the suspects, noisy and disoriented as they came out of the woods. They would know more after the suspects had been questioned.

"Well," said Scott admiringly, "you guys certainly know how to have adventures!"

Charles and Loki looked doubtfully at each other before Charles answered. "I hope you don't ever have adventures like these."

Scott's spirits weren't dampened and he nodded enthusiastically at Charles, then went to help someone who'd arrived in the store. Keeley's phone chimed with a text. "Declan," she said. "He wants to talk to you, Charles. OK if he comes over?"

"Of course," said Charles, who was beginning to realize how wonderful it was to not carry everything alone.

Declan arrived quickly. Rory came with him.

"Not again, Charles, for heaven's sake," smiled Declan. "You've got the luck of the Irish!"

They all laughed and the story was told again. But Declan and Rory had come for a different reason.

"A feast is what we need," said Declan. "It's almost Christmas and Rory and I are thinking we'll do a big spread at our place on Christmas Eve. We have lots to celebrate. We've all been through a lot this year…" he faltered and Rory took over.

"We do indeed have a lot to celebrate," Rory said. "Here we all are healthy, safe and together and we need a feast. So there would be all of us, of course. And we're going to ask the Itos, Yvonne and Peter, Elizabeth, Luc Gagnon and his family, Tom Williams and his family and maybe even Maren Quayle." He threw a quick look at Charles, who pointedly avoided responding. "Declan and I know her well. We'll all promise not to talk shop so the police and lawyers won't have to worry. We can potluck it. Declan will provide the music. I will provide the beer and wine."

"And I," said Charles, getting into the spirit of it all, "will commission a series of Christmas desserts from Peter and his crew—cakes, puddings, shortbread and chocolate logs." They all looked delightedly at each other and Charles realized he'd taken the last step. He belonged here. Cascade Canyon was his new home.

They sat for a long time planning and chatting, with Keeley and the students leaving from time to time to help customers. Then Charles left to talk with Peter about desserts. Rory and Declan went with him to invite Yvonne and Peter to the feast.

By the time Loki and Charles were back home, gear stowed, hiking clothes in the washing machine and beer in hand, Declan had reported to them that almost everyone had accepted the invitation to the feast. Maren Quayle said she would wait to accept her invitation until she'd had a chance to question the men who'd shot at Charles and Loki, to make sure there was no conflict of interest.

Luc stopped by to check on Charles and Loki and refused to be drawn into answering any questions. He asked them to come to the RCMP detachment first thing the following morning to talk about the arrest of the men who'd ambushed them. He was off duty and they were glad when he accepted a beer and joined them in Loki's comfortable den. They talked about Rory's and Declan's Christmas feast, whether or not Loki was planning any new expeditions, how Luc's wife, Sara, a music teacher at the local elementary school, was organizing the school Christmas concert, and they debated the merits of Canadian vs English beer. Murder and mayhem were off the table.

The RCMP detachment was in the busy, built-up centre of North Vancouver. Charles and Loki reported to the front desk and were taken into a small, plain room at the back with just four chairs and a table. They sat down to wait and soon Luc came in with Maren Quayle. She came straight over to Charles and sat beside him.

"Mr. Deeds," she said sympathetically. "I'm so sorry for all you've been through since you came to Cascade Canyon. I hope we'll be able to work towards some kind of resolution for you. Nothing can change the past, but finding the truth can help change the present and the future."

Charles, surprised but guarded, nodded at her and said nothing.

Loki spoke to her. "Mrs. Quayle, it sounds as if you don't consider Charles a suspect any more. Is that right?"

"Yes, that's right," she said and Charles bowed his head in relief and looked away.

"We believe you're a target, Mr. Deeds," she said. "You've been attacked twice now. I think someone wants to stop you from remembering what happened when you went to see Sayer Mason on the night he was killed."

Charles shook his head in frustration. "I keep trying to remember but it's just a complete blank."

Maren looked at him sympathetically. "Give it time."

She paused. "There's something else. I know you left the book and the letter in Cascade Canyon when you went to Portland."

Charles looked startled. "How do you…?

"Corporal Gagnon told me you'd given him a copy of the letter and I…"

Charles cut in, speaking directly to Luc. "You gave your word, Gagnon, that you would show no one the letter," he said angrily.

"Mr. Deeds," Maren interjected, "I have not seen the letter. I simply asked Corporal Gagnon if he knew where it was and he told me it was safe here in Cascade Canyon."

Charles looked at her doubtfully. Then he muttered an apology to Luc, but his heart wasn't in it. "Why do you need to know where the letter is?" he asked. "What does it matter?"

Maren answered. "I asked Corporal Gagnon about it when you first came back from Portland because I needed to know whether your attacker got the book and the letter the night Sayer Mason was murdered. But now someone has taken shots at you here in Cascade Canyon. Knowing you still have the book and the letter means that they either want to retrieve those or they want to stop you from remembering that night in Portland. Possibly both."

Luc jumped in, not the affable neighbour they'd shared a beer with last night, but the professional police officer. "We still don't know where you're hiding the book and the letter, Mr. Deeds. We're willing to overlook you dodging us and heading to Portland that night because Tom Williams has explained that you were in a state of shock and did nothing wrong. But if the book and the letter are dangerous I need to know you're not putting lives at risk again by keeping it hidden."

Charles looked at him defiantly.

Then Loki said, "Makes sense."

Charles looked at his friend and let his anger go. "Will you allow me to step outside to make a short phone call?" he asked Luc and Maren.

Maren looked at Luc. "Five minutes," Luc said. "And Loki, go with him. Don't leave the building, either of you."

It took less than five minutes. Maren and Luc looked expectantly at Charles as he and Loki came back in.

"If you'll both come with me now to a place in Cascade Canyon," said Charles, "we'll retrieve the book and the letter and take them to the safe in Folios."

Luc leapt up. "Let's go!" he said.

"Wait," said Maren. "Mr. Deeds and Mr. Andresson, first we want to update you on our investigation into the two men who shot at you. They're Americans. They work in security at the Portland branch of Mason Conglomerate. They're known to police but have kept out of trouble for several years now. They won't tell us who hired them. It seems to us that they're scared, which is interesting, because if Sayer Mason was responsible for trying to steal the book when Declan was hurt and was also responsible for the attack on you in Portland, Mr. Deeds, he's dead now and can't hurt them. What, or who are they afraid of now?"

They all sat for a moment, lost in thought as Maren's words sank in. If Sayer Mason wasn't the instigator of all this, who was? There was still a murderer out there, still a threat. And no one knew where to start looking.

Maren got to her feet. "That's all we know for now but we're working hard to find out more. Let's go and get the book."

Kaito Ito was waiting for them. He bowed to each of them in turn, reserving his longest bow for Maren Quayle. Then he ushered them into his workshop. Maren and Luc looked around curiously. They knew the book had found its way to Past Life after being in the Itos' possession for many years.

Kaito went to where his finished pottery was stored. On the ground stood a lidded pot, glazed in rich green, the colour of the deep forest. He looked at Charles, who nodded. Kaito opened the lid and reached inside, lifting out the book covered in the ancient linen cloth. Kaito went to Charles and with a deep bow, handed him the book.

"Arigatou gozaimashita, Ito-san," said Charles, his voice full of emotion as he returned the bow.

"This is it," said Charles to Maren and Luc. "I asked Mr. Ito to take care of it for me. You both know that although the Itos have a part in the story of the book they have nothing to do with what's happening now. I knew no one would ever come looking for it here. I asked Mr. Ito to keep it here and tell no one until I asked for it back."

He handed the book, still wrapped in the cloth, to Maren Quayle. She took it carefully. "May I unwrap it?" she asked Charles.

"Yes," he said.

She unwrapped it and gazed at the cover for a moment, spellbound. Luc came to stand beside her. The book still held a strange power. They could feel the ripple of ancient energy in the room. Kaito put his hand on his potter's wheel, as if to steady himself.

"So this is where it's been hiding," said Luc, a little awestruck. "This is what it's all been about." He didn't reach for it. "Where's the letter?"

"It's in the lining of the book," said Charles. "I have the instruments I need at Folios to extract it again without harming the book."

Maren held the book and the cloth out to Charles. "Let's go to Folios," she said.

Charles took the book with both hands and held it against his heart for a moment. Then he quickly took the cloth from Maren and wrapped it around the book again, as if to smother its power.

They all thanked Kaito Ito, who said he would see them at Declan's and Rory's party.

In Luc's squad car they went down the back lane to Folios. They got up the steps to the bookshop without seeing anyone. Loki put the 'closed' sign on the front door and led them into the back room where they sat around the worktable. Slowly and carefully Charles extracted the letter from Carter's book. They could all see it gave him pain just to touch it. He handed it to Maren Quayle, still folded.

"I can't bear to read it again yet," he said. "But I think I know it by heart and I'll try to answer your questions."

They sat in silence as Maren read it. After she'd finished she closed her eyes for a moment, then looked at Charles. "Mr. Deeds," she said gently. "I've been thinking about this letter only as evidence, but to see it with my own eyes…I offer you my deepest and most sincere sympathy on all your losses and the grief this has released. I don't see the need for us to keep this. It will be safer locked away here at Folios. Corporal Gagnon, please take photographs."

Luc did as she asked, using his phone, taking photos of every page of the letter and a few of the book.

Then Maren said, "Mr. Deeds, we're looking at a murder in this letter, you know that. It took place a hundred years ago, but it's a murder nonetheless. We have a confession here."

"Yes," said Charles. "There's no doubt. He says he buried her where…" his voice broke and he couldn't go on.

Loki came to his rescue. "What happens next?" he asked. "This took place in the distant past. Do you really need to pursue it now? Can't we just leave it in the past where it belongs?"

Maren spoke. "But it hasn't stayed in the past, Mr. Andresson. The repercussions of this letter have travelled from that dreadful day in Watertown to the present day in Cascade Canyon, as well as to Portland and who knows where else? We have no choice but to investigate further."

Charles recovered his voice. "You're absolutely right Mrs. Quayle," he said. "We need to find out everything we can about this. It's the only way there will ever be peace for all the lost and troubled souls whose lives have been affected by the events of a century ago. I will welcome it, solving all the mysteries, challenging all the lies, finding out once and for all who is still prepared to kill to keep this letter from ever seeing the light of day."

He put the letter back into the lining of the book, wrapped the book in the linen cloth and went with Loki to lock it in the safe.

"The question now is," said Maren to Luc. "Where do we start?"

CHAPTER
TWENTY-THREE

On the evening of December 24, Charles walked with Keeley and Loki to Rory's and Declan's house. The house was covered with lights and the front door was open. Declan stood there with a Santa hat on his head and a twinkle in his eye. "Come on in, dear ones!" he said and ushered them inside.

In the living room a massive Christmas tree with decorations and tinsel thick on its branches reached the tall ceiling. The scent of pine filled the air and logs crackled in the fireplace, throwing a shimmering red cast onto the brick mantelpiece. Candles were everywhere, sending shadows dancing around the room. There was no electric light. Vivaldi played softly in the background and for a moment, Charles felt as if he'd stepped back to an earlier place and time.

The students were already there, clustered around the table in the adjoining dining room, eating the appetizers they'd brought. Keeley took her turkey casserole to the kitchen and put it in the oven to warm. Loki put his dish on the table. "It's Ribbe," he said. "Pork belly with sauer-kraut and redcurrant sauce. Recipe handed down from my Norwegian bestemor, my grandmother." He beamed at them proudly and they gathered round to praise the dish.

Rory came into the room with a bottle of red wine. "Glasses are on the table, there's beer on ice in the kitchen and cold drinks in the fridge if you'd rather." He held up the bottle to Charles. "Can I pour you one Charles?"

"I'd love a glass, thank you!" said Charles. He looked and felt calm and happy and everyone who'd been watching him for signs of stress relaxed.

Elizabeth Liang leapt up from her chair by the fire. "Charles!" she said. "Come and tell me everything!" She took his hand and led him to a chair next to hers. They were soon lost in conversation.

A knock on the door announced the arrival of Peter and Yvonne. Peter carried several exciting boxes and trays. "The puddings and pastries you ordered, Charles," he said, "and a few cream horns for good measure!" Everyone laughed and Peter strode happily into the kitchen.

The Itos arrived shortly after Peter and Yvonne. They'd brought Japanese pancakes and beef tataki to add to the feast.

Everyone gravitated towards the fire. Some sat in the comfy chairs, others stood and chatted and the buzz of happy conversation filled the room. Declan kept the music mellow and seasonal, moving from Vivaldi to Chopin to Handel.

"Just heard from Tom that he and his family are on the way, so we'll start dinner soon," said Rory.

Tom and his wife and three children brought baked salmon and a huge pot of mashed potatoes. "My kids eat like horses," Tom joked. Tom's wife Elaine knew everyone except Charles so introductions were made. While Charles was talking to Elaine, their youngest and only daughter suddenly put her hand in his and looked up at him with all the pure delight of a fearless little child. He looked down, surprised, and a great leap of joy filled his heart. "You talk different," she said in her sweet voice, muffled by two missing front teeth.

"Tasha," said Elaine gently, but Charles was quick to answer. "I do," he said. "I'm from England. And you're a very smart girl to notice." Her huge smile said it all and she went to find her brothers with a toss of her head.

By the time Luc and his wife Sara arrived with their two children the party was in full swing. Rory and Declan had set up the den with Christmas movies, board games and art supplies. The kids, who all went to school together, went off in high spirits.

"Let's get dinner going," said Rory. "Could everyone be responsible for getting the dish they brought on the table, please, then load your plates and just perch anywhere you like. I'll be refilling wine for those who are drinking it and everyone else help yourselves!"

The crowd moved towards the table. Charles held back, needing a moment to take in all the joy he was feeling.

There was a knock on the door. Charles glanced at Rory, who was by the dining room table giving orders and hadn't heard the knock.

Charles hesitated. What if it was trouble? But he shook off the spasm of fear and threw his trust into the happiness and security of the moment. He opened the door.

Maren Quayle stood there with a bottle of champagne in her hand. Her hair, brushed to the side and held with a sparkling clip, shone like silver. Her dress was midnight blue silk and as she stepped into the room it gleamed and shimmered in the candlelight. Charles was speechless. He'd only seen her before in tense and formal circumstances and he suddenly saw her in a new light, warm, lovely and sophisticated. "Mrs. Quayle," he said, "I hope you won't mind me saying how lovely you look. Please come in."

"It's Maren, Mr. Deeds" she said with a smile. "And I will always be grateful for a genuine compliment."

"Then it's Charles," he said. "May I?" He offered her his arm and she took it. All heads turned towards them as they walked to the table. Conversation stopped. Declan, who knew Maren well, quickly stepped in to save her any awkwardness. "Maren!" he said. "How lovely, my dear fellow music lover! Come on to the table and let's get you some dinner."

She stepped away from Charles and he missed having her by his side. He shook off the sentimentality, putting it down to the wine, the candles and the happy gathering, but she looked back at him and smiled and he knew there would be more to their story.

By the time the last cream horn had disappeared and the children were sprawled around the den watching *Elf,* the adults had all found themselves comfy chairs in cozy nooks around the big living room. Conversations were quiet, punctuated by happy laughter and the occasional pronouncement on the glory of the feast.

As Rory heaped more wood on the fire, Declan pulled up a chair beside it and got his guitar out. A ripple of delight went through the room. Declan sang carols, sweet and soft. The old ones—*The Holly and the Ivy, God Rest Ye Merry Gentlemen, In the Bleak Midwinter.* The children, feeling the ancient pull of songs sung by a fireside, came to sit on the floor beside the adults. Little Tasha sat down on the floor beside Charles's chair and edged towards him until she was leaning against his knee. He looked down at her and she smiled up at him. It was painfully sweet and moving for him to experience such trust. He smiled back at her then quickly looked away, his eyes filling with tears. He recovered to see Maren looking at him with compassion in her eyes. She nodded almost imperceptibly and he knew she understood what he was feeling and why.

Declan rounded off the evening with *Wild Mountain Thyme.* While not a carol, it lent itself so sweetly to his lovely Irish voice that everyone felt it a fitting finale.

Tom, Elaine, Luc and Sara roused their children, said goodnight and Merry Christmas and headed for the door, carrying the sleepy youngest ones in their arms. Peter and Yvonne declared that they would love to walk Mr. and Mrs. Ito home on such a fine night. Keeley, Loki, Elizabeth and the students, who'd all helped to tidy everything up after dinner, headed up the road in a happy group. Once again Charles offered his arm to Maren, who gladly accepted. As they left, Charles looked back to see Rory and Declan at their front door, Rory's arm thrown around Declan's shoulders, their glasses of brandy raised in farewell and good wishes for the season. Charles and Maren waved back.

"Merry Christmas Maren," Charles said as they walked away and up the road.

"Merry Christmas Charles," she replied. She leaned in to him and he held her close against the cold.

CHAPTER
TWENTY-FOUR

The new year began and with fair weather on the horizon the people of Cascade Canyon had their annual spring cleaning, searching through cupboards, basements and attics for things to give away. Past Life was the main beneficiary of this effort. Keeley, Rory, Declan and the students had their hands full sorting, shelving and recycling. In some cases Keeley checked with the people who'd dropped things off to make sure they'd really meant to give away the vintage Sadler Henry VIII teapot or the art deco silver filagree necklace. The answer was always yes. Past Life's generous support of the women's shelter and the elementary school were well known and people were glad that the things they no longer wanted or needed would become someone else's loved possessions and help the community at the same time. So there were many treasures, but no more old books, ancient linen cloths, hidden letters.

Charles was still staying at Loki's apartment. They had become firm friends, having much in common. They'd shared a few winter adventures on North Shore trails since the time they were ambushed and had plans for some ambitious spring hikes. There had been no further incidents, no trouble, no threats, no break-ins. The case had gone cold, as Luc said, frustrated by the lack of progress both in Cascade Canyon and in Portland.

Charles declared his intention of buying his own place. Loki assured him that there was no rush but Charles was ready to make a full commitment to building a new life in Cascade Canyon. The time he was spending with Maren had become an unexpected joy for both of them. She knew the village well and was helping him to find a place. He'd surprised himself by realizing that he wanted a little house, not an apartment.

In early January the perfect place came on the market and he and Maren went to see it. It was at the far end of the village, up against the forest, within walking distance of everyone and everything he'd come to know in Cascade Canyon. The Renfrews, an elderly couple who'd lived there for fifty years, had decided to spent their golden years in a warmer climate. Their home had once been one of the old ski cabins, built in the 1940s after the new Lions Gate Bridge opened the North Shore to all who loved mountain adventures.

The cabin was built from massive cedar logs. Over the years it had been modernized, added to and landscaped— but inside, some of the walls still exposed the burnished yellow logs, while others were covered by hand-split cedar shakes. Polished pine shelves and cupboards, hardwood floors and high ceilings gave the place light and space.

There were three bedrooms and a good-sized living room with a stone fireplace. It was a perfect example of a well-appointed mid-century cabin, but when you stepped into the kitchen that notion fell away instantly. The kitchen was sparkling steel and glass with the latest appliances and a generous island countertop, above which a pine hanging rack held gleaming copper pots and pans.

Charles knew instantly he'd found his new home. He offered what the Renfrews were asking and closed the deal the same day. As Charles and Maren sat with the Renfrews over a cup of tea in the living room, Mr. Renfrew asked Charles if there was anything in the cabin he'd like to keep, as there wasn't much room where they were going. Charles looked at Maren for advice.

"What about the copper pots and the hanging rack in the kitchen?" she asked Charles, who nodded eagerly.

"Of course," said Mr. Renfrew. "Good choice."

"And are any of the rugs available?" Maren asked. She and Charles had both noticed the beautiful hooked and braided rugs scattered throughout the cabin.

"They are!" said Mrs. Renfrew.

They settled on a price for the copper pots and the rugs and everyone was pleased with the outcome.

As they walked down the cabin's gravel driveway towards the village's main street, Charles suddenly pulled Maren into a hug. "This is all so wonderful and right," he said.

"It is, Charles," said Maren. "It's perfect."

The Renfrews moved out at the end of January and Charles sent a team of painters, a structural engineer, a plumber and an electrician to the cabin to make sure everything was safe and shipshape. The structural engineer declared that the house would stand solidly for another hundred years.

Charles decided to furnish the place, as much as possible, with items from Past Life. It became both a challenge and an adventure for Keeley, Declan, Rory and the students to find the perfect armchairs, dining room and kitchen sets, occasional tables, lamps and many more eclectic items for the cabin. As soon as they were approved by Charles, Keeley put a 'sold' sign on them.

On one of Charles's visits to the store, Arwen came to talk to him. "You must have a housewarming, Charles," she said. "We all want to see your new home and celebrate with you."

"I hadn't thought of it, but it's a lovely idea," Charles said. He had great affection for Arwen, who'd always shown him compassion and kindness. "I'm planning to move in on the first of March, all being well."

She was thrilled. "We'll all help to organize it," she declared, "as soon as you're moved in and settled." She went off to tell the others the news.

As Arwen left for the back room, Luc and Tom came through the front door.

"I thought we might find you here, Charles," said Luc.

Charles tensed as all the old fears and trauma came flooding back.

"What is it?" he asked. "What's happened?"

"It's the inquest," said Tom. "The inquest into Sayer Mason's death. They've set a date. Reid Summers just contacted me to let me know you'll be called as a witness."

Charles had gone pale and Tom reached out to steady him. "Why don't we go into the back room," he said.

They walked into the back room, where Arwen was excitely telling Keeley, Rory and Declan about the housewarming. She broke off mid-sentence when she saw the look on Charles's face.

"Would you all mind if we have the room for a few minutes?" asked Tom.

They all moved to the door, but Declan stopped next to Charles.

"We'll be right in there if you need us, Charles," he said. "Just call out for us."

Charles nodded, numbly. He couldn't think. He was back in a dark place full of old books, letters, blindness and tragedy.

"Let's sit down," said Tom, gently.

"I'll get us some coffee," said Luc.

Tom spoke again and Charles looked up, shaking himself out of the fog. "The inquest is set for February 16," said Tom. "You'll need to be there the day before so Reid can brief you. I'll do everything I can to help prepare you at this end."

Luc brought the coffee back to the table and said to Charles, "I've asked Detective Santos to keep me in the loop with the latest evidence and anything they think might come up at the inquest. As much as I can, Charles, I'll keep you informed."

Charles looked at Luc and nodded his thanks. They'd come a long way since their adversarial first days.

"Oh no," Charles said, suddenly and they both looked at him, alarmed. "I'm supposed to be moving into my new cabin on the first of March. How will I manage it all?"

Tom smiled. "Haven't you learned yet, Charles, that in Cascade Canyon no one needs to do anything all on their own?"

They all laughed and the tension was broken. Hearing them, Declan put his head round the door. "Can we come back in?" he asked.

"Sure," said Luc. "Charles will fill you in."

Tom and Luc stood up to leave.

"Can you come and see me in my office tomorrow, Charles?" Tom asked. "We'll go over everything. This is all going to be OK. Don't worry. Between Reid and me you'll have all the preparation and support you need."

After Tom and Luc left Charles told them all what had happened.

"Don't worry about your cabin," said Rory. "We'll all help you. It will be fine."

"And we'll have the housewarming when you get back," said Arwen. "Scott and Sherine and I will organize everything!"

Keeley spoke then, after listening quietly to them all. "I'm going with you Charles…no…don't try to talk me out of it. I'm going. And I'm sure Loki will want to go too."

Charles reached for her hand. "What can I say?" He looked around at them. "Thank you, all of you. My friends."

Keeley spoke for them all. "We were there at the beginning of this, Charles and we'll be there with you to see it through to the end."

The door between the front room and the back suddenly slammed shut and they all looked at it, startled.

"It's nothing, just the wind coming under the back door," said Keeley. But it wasn't the first time she'd felt as if something ancient, ethereal and awake had brushed them all with its icy breath.

CHAPTER
TWENTY-FIVE

On the morning of February 15, Charles, Keeley and Loki boarded a plane for Portland. Loki had booked them all into the hotel where he and Keeley had stayed last time. No one voiced their feelings of deja-vu but they all felt it.

Reid Summers was waiting for them at Portland International. He took them to the hotel, waited while Charles checked in and took him to his office downtown, promising to have him back by dinner time.

Keeley and Loki, with the afternoon to themselves, headed straight for Powell's and spent the time immersed in the comforting world of books. Keeley found a book about old ski cabins in the Pacific Northwest and bought it as a housewarming gift for Charles. Loki liked the idea of getting Charles a book to celebrate his new house and purchased *Forgotten Things: The Story of the Seymour Valley Archaeology Project* by Bob Muckle, professor and archaeologist. It was about the Japanese village Mr. Ito had told them about, lost long ago in the forests of North Vancouver.

At dinner time they headed back to the hotel to find Charles waiting for them at a quiet table in the corner of the bar with an untouched beer in front of him. They were relieved to see that he looked calm. He smiled when he saw them.

"Let me get you a drink," Charles said. "It's quiet here and I can tell you what Reid said."

Once their drinks had arrived, Charles filled them in.

"Reid made me feel quite confident," he said. "He assured me that I'm absolutely not a suspect and that my testimony shouldn't be complicated. I'll just tell them why I went to see Mason, what happened while I was there and what I remember, which isn't very much, about leaving."

"Sounds straightforward," said Loki. "Will Keeley and I be allowed to attend or is it closed?"

"You'll be able to come, thank goodness," said Charles. "Reid told me a bit about the proceedings. The whole thing is run by the district attorney. There will be a six member panel, a jury essentially. There will also be a number of witnesses—the police, the Chief Medical Examiner, the housekeeper…" Charles looked down, apprehension in his voice, "and members of Mason's family."

"You'll be alright Charles," said Keeley. "We'll be there. You can focus on us and not the pain that family has caused you."

"It's going to take more than one day to hear all those witnesses, isn't it?" said Loki. "Good thing we planned to stay for a while."

Charles nodded. "Reid said they probably won't even get to me tomorrow but I should still be there, just in case."

They took Charles to Mother's Bistro, which he loved, and proved it by ordering a hearty meal. For a few hours they put all their worries behind them and simply enjoyed good food and good conversation in good company.

Charles said goodnight to them at the door of their hotel room. "Bright and early tomorrow!" he said. "My father always used to say that to me. Funny, I haven't thought about it for years."

Keeley's and Loki's room had a kitchen and a living room. They sat together on the sofa, lights dim, sipping wine that Loki had bought earlier.

"Here we are again," he said, putting his arm around her. She put her head on his shoulder and they sat quietly for a while, until Loki put their wine glasses on the side table, took her hand and took her to bed.

The uproar outside the courtroom was overwhelming. People were jostling for places in the line to get into the public gallery, television cameras were everywhere, reporters were yelling out questions to everyone who looked official, police were holding back two groups of protesters, and men who looked like private security guards were shielding several people who were trying to get inside. Both Charles and Loki put their arms around Keeley as they tried to get through the crowd. Then Reid Summers was there, head and shoulders above most of the crowd, clearing a path towards the courtroom door in no uncertain terms. He got them inside and closed the door behind them.

"Wow," he said, "I knew it would be a circus but this is crazy. Sayer Mason was a celebrity, a crook or a successful business magnate, depending on where you stand. There's huge public interest in this case."

He ushered them to an area at the back of the main floor underneath the public gallery, where they could watch proceedings without drawing attention to themselves. They could hear the public gallery filling up noisily above their heads. The ground floor gradually filled too, with officials, jury panel members and others. They recognized Detective Santos, who glanced around, nodded to them without smiling then took a seat near the front.

When the room was almost full a side door opened and several people came in, surrounded by the private security guards.

"The Mason family," said Reid in a low tone.

The family sat near the front and did not look round. Charles was surprised that he felt an odd ripple of sympathy for them. They had, after all, lost their father.

Reid went to sit with Detective Santos as the court clerk got to her feet to call for silence. The proceedings were presided over by District Attorney the Honorable Mr. Torrin Bell. Reid had told Charles that Bell had a reputation for fairness and no-nonsense. The D.A. took his seat and described the process, explaining that he would swear in the jury panel and inform them of their duties, then he would question the witnesses. The jury members would have an opportunity to question the witnesses too, if they wished, as would the lawyers.

Keeley, Loki and Charles looked at each other. It was going to be a long process.

D.A. Bell called the first witness, Detective Santos.

Detective Santos described the police response to the shooting. Then she told the court that on the previous day, after hearing from the RCMP that Charles Deeds might be a threat to Sayer Mason, the Oregon police had put a watch on the border and the airport and had contacted Mason and told him to be alert. He'd brushed them off, insisting that he had excellent security and was used to people who threatened him with various things. Detective Santos went on to say that when Charles Deeds regained consciousness after being hospitalized with a head injury she'd interviewed him and determined that he was a victim, not a suspect and that currently there were no suspects.

A murmur of angry dissent ran through the Mason family and D.A. Bell looked sternly in their direction, with a frown and a slight shake of his head. He explained that they would all hear from Charles Deeds in due course. Two of the men in the Mason group looked around the courtroom, scrutinizing the crowd.

Beside her, Keeley felt Charles tense. He glanced anxiously at Reid in his seat at the front, but Reid purposefully looked straight ahead. He doesn't want to identify Charles, Keeley thought, suddenly. No one knows who he is.

After Detective Santos, D.A. Bell called several police officers, the chief medical examiner and the Mason family doctor to make their statements. For Charles, Keeley and Loki, these testimonies added nothing new to what Luc, Tom and Reid had already told them.

When the lunch break was declared they left quickly, before the public gallery could empty. Reid joined them as they picked up sandwiches and coffee and led them to the back of the courthouse, where they perched on a wall out of sight of reporters and the curious public. Not much was said. They could see that Charles was lost in his own thoughts and didn't press him. After lunch, Reid showed them a back way into the courtroom and they managed to get to their seats without a problem.

As soon as there was quiet in the courtroom, D.A. Bell called Hewitt Carradine. A distinguished, silver-haired man separated himself from the Mason family group, walked towards the witness box and confirmed his name.

"He's the Mason family lawyer," Loki reminded Keeley in a quiet voice. "The one who found Sayer Mason."

The District Attorney spoke. "Mr. Carradine, tell us please, about your involvement in the events of the night Sayer Mason died."

Hewitt Carradine had a powerful speaking voice. Keeley imagined what a daunting opponent he would be in court and out of it. His voice carried clearly to the back of the room. "Sayer Mason phoned me just after 9:00 p.m. on the night of October 28," he said. "He told me that a man, Charles Deeds, had been to see him. He said that Deeds had threatened to expose a letter that would be damaging to the entire Mason family and particularly to Sayer Mason's chances of being elected to public office."

Charles, who'd been looking down, sat bolt upright. This time it was Loki who murmured something in his ear that seemed to reassure him.

Carradine continued. "Sayer told me he'd seen a copy of the letter and had sent Deeds away to get the original. He said he had told Deeds that once he had the original and could see that it was authentic they could discuss the best thing to do. I asked him where Deeds was now and he said he had left. Then he asked me to come over to the mansion. We had several things to discuss and I'd been planning to go and see him anyway, even before he called."

"So Sayer Mason was alive after Charles Deeds left?" asked the D.A.

"He was, although Deeds might have returned," Carradine said.

Reid murmured and started to get to his feet but the District Attorney waved at him to sit down.

"Mr. Carradine, you know better than to speculate," Bell said.

Carradine nodded but held the District Attorney's gaze unwaveringly. Bell spoke. "And what did you do then, Mr. Carradine?"

"I spent a bit of time organizing the papers I was taking to Sayer, got in my car and drove to the mansion. I knocked on the front door and found that it wasn't closed. I was alarmed. I called out to Sayer and heard nothing, so I went to look for him."

"What did you find?" asked Bell.

For the first time, Hewitt Carradine faltered. "Sayer was… he was in his study. He had fallen across his desk. He'd been shot and there was… there was a lot of blood. I felt for a pulse but there was nothing. So I called 9-1-1. The police came fast because they'd been nearby at a motor vehicle accident. I'd come upon the accident on my way to the mansion but emergency services were already there so I just drove on."

Loki whispered to Charles. *"The road accident, that must have been you."* Charles looked back at Loki, shocked. It was overwhelming. Why couldn't he remember? He closed his eyes and concentrated, willing himself to think back but it was still a complete blank. Then he was aware that Torrin Bell was speaking again.

"What time did you get to the mansion, Mr. Carradine?" asked Bell.

"It was at about 10:30, I think. The police can verify the time," said Carradine.

Bell pursued the details. "Was there anyone else around, Mr. Carradine—in the house, in the grounds, on the road?"

"Not that I know of," said Carradine. "The police searched the house and grounds but there was nothing."

"I know this is hard, sir, as you've known Sayer Mason for a very long time," said the District Attorney, "but is there anything else you can add, any information, any threats, any grievances you're aware of that might have resulted in this murder?"

Hewitt Carradine looked at the Mason family and seemed to be considering something, but he thought better of it. "No," he said, "there's nothing I can add. It would only be speculation and that won't help any of us."

Keeley, Charles and Loki looked at each other, deeply curious about what Carradine was holding back.

It was late in the afternoon and there was one more witness for the day. Mason's housekeeper was called. Charles sat up in his seat and strained to hear. This was someone he remembered.

The housekeeper had been sitting a few seats away from the family, obviously not included in their protection. She was young, in her twenties, with blond hair pulled into a loose bun. She seemed to be on the verge of tears and the District Attorney tried to reassure her.

"Please state your name," he said. "Just take the time you need."

She said her name so quietly that they couldn't hear her at the back.

"Miss McLean," said Torrin Bell, "you were Sayer Mason's housekeeper. How long were you in that position?"

She whispered a reply.

"Please speak up so we can all hear, Miss McLean," said Bell.

She tried. "Two years," she said.

"And did you live at the Mason mansion?"

"No, I live downtown, near the river."

"Can you tell us what you remember of the night Sayer Mason was killed? Tell us what you were doing."

She looked at District Attorney Bell rather than the crowd, seeming to draw courage from him.

"I worked late that night," she said. "Mr. Mason asked me to get his dinner ready and take it in on a tray because he was expecting someone."

"Do you know who he was expecting?"

"No but Mr. Ryker and Mr. Jack were there just about every evening so I thought it was probably them."

"So you took Mr. Mason's dinner in to him. What happened then?"

"Well, I was just getting ready to go home when there was a knock on the front door. I thought it was strange because Mr. Ryker and Mr. Jack have keys and no one else ever just shows up at the mansion without calling first. But I went to answer it."

"Who was it."

"It was a man from England...he talked like he was from England. Mr. Deeds." She paused, looked around, spotted Charles at the back and pointed. "That man there."

In one motion the Mason family and all their security people turned to look at where she was pointing. But Charles sat perfectly still and gave nothing away so they couldn't be sure who he was. They muttered to each other until D.A. Bell asked for silence.

"Please go on, Miss McLean," Bell said.

The housekeeper glanced quickly at the Mason family and went on. "Well, he seemed really upset, but he was very polite to me and asked if it would be possible to see Mr. Mason. I said I didn't think he would see him because it was late, but he said to tell Mr. Mason his name was Charles Deeds and then he would see him. I didn't ask him in and he didn't try to come in. I went back to tell Mr. Mason about it."

"What happened then?" Bell asked.

"Well it was really strange," she said. "When I told Mr. Mason his name it was like it was a bad surprise for him. Then Mr. Mason came with me to the front door, which he never did. He said, 'Go home' to me, like he was angry, so I quickly went back to the kitchen to get my purse. By the time I got back to the front door to leave they were in Mr. Mason's study. Mr. Mason was shouting at Mr. Deeds. I was a bit scared and I didn't want to get involved so I left the house and drove away."

"What time was that, Miss McLean?" Bell asked. "Do you remember?"

"I remember looking at my watch when I got in my car and thinking that the grocery store I usually go to would be closed and I'd only missed it by a few minutes. So it must have been just after 8:30."

"Is there anything else you can tell us? Did you see anyone else?" Bell asked.

"No, I was just anxious to get home. I didn't see anyone else come to the mansion."

Torrin Bell spoke again. "Thank you, Miss McLean. Do any members of the jury panel or other Counsels have any questions for this witness?"

Reid Summers stood up. "I do," he said.

Keeley put her hand on Charles's arm. He was rigid with tension, staring at Reid and the witness as if willing himself to remember the events of that night.

"Miss McLean," said Reid. "I represent Charles Deeds. When he came to the door that night did you feel threatened by him or afraid?"

"No sir," she said, "I felt sorry for him. He was so polite and he looked so sad."

"And did you hear Mr. Deeds shouting back at Mr. Mason?"

"No sir, there was only Mr. Mason shouting."

"Thank you Miss McLean," said Reid. He turned to the jury. "I'd like to have it read into the record that police both here and in Canada have found no reason to consider my client, Charles Deeds, a suspect. He'll be appearing as a witness on a voluntary basis later in these proceedings." He sat down.

A few curious heads turned to look around the room but Charles sat with his head down, so they quickly gave up. Keeley noticed one of the Mason family turn and scan the room again. One of the sons, she wondered? She couldn't decide who was security and who was family. They all looked too tough to tangle with. Like Charles, she had decided not to watch the news coverage of Sayer Mason's funeral so she didn't recognize anyone. She knew they'd find out soon enough.

At the end of the day District Attorney Bell called a halt to proceedings and advised them all to return the following morning at nine sharp. The jury was escorted out by the side door and following them, blocked and protected by their security detail, the Mason family left.

Keeley, Loki and Charles stood up and stretched. Reid came back to talk to them. "You'll be one of the first witnesses tomorrow, Charles, after the Mason brothers," he said.

Charles nodded. "I'm ready. Thanks Reid."

Reid arranged to pick them all up at the hotel in the morning and said goodbye.

"Shall we take a walk before dinner?" asked Loki. "I think it would do us all good."

They walked in silence beside the beautiful Willamette River with the sunlight dipping towards evening, through woods with carpets of leaves still touched by frost. Then Charles stopped and smiled, pointing down at the ground where tiny new shoots pushed through the dead leaves, the resilient first signs of spring, a promise of new life that never failed.

CHAPTER TWENTY-SIX

By quarter to nine the next morning they were back in the courtroom. This time they sat at the front. Reid sat in the front row beside Charles. Keeley and Loki sat in the row behind them. At nine sharp District Attorney Bell convened proceedings and called the first witness, Ryker Mason.

The man who took the stand was dressed in a dark business suit. Keeley guessed he was in his mid-thirties. He was tall, with dark hair, and dark eyes filled with pain and sadness. It would be easy to underestimate this man, thought Keeley, but she could see the fire in him. She wondered if he was as ambitious and ruthless as his father. That remained to be seen.

"Mr. Mason," said Torrin Bell, "please tell us what you remember of the night your father was killed."

Ryker's voice broke when he started to talk but he paused, pulled his shoulders back and fixed the D.A. with a frank and open gaze. When he spoke again his voice was clear and strong with an almost imperceptible edge of anger.

"Hewitt called me," he said, looking towards where his family sat. "Hewitt Carradine, our lawyer. He called me and said that Father had been… had been shot." He took a deep breath and continued. "He said that Father had asked him to come and see him to talk about the business." He looked at the jury, explaining, "We were in the process of devolving the business away from Father to Jack and myself, as Father prepared to take public office. He was going to give each of us half of Mason Conglomerate."

Charles glanced at Reid. This was different from Hewitt Carradine's testimony. Charles guessed that Carradine was covering up the existence of the letter at the time and had given Ryker another reason for his visit that night.

"And what did you do?"

"I called my brother Jack. I couldn't reach him so I left a message telling him to come to the mansion urgently. Then I got in my car and drove to the mansion as fast as I could. By the time I got there the paramedics were there— and the police. They'd all been close by attending to a road accident so they were able to get there fast. But there was nothing they could do. Father was dead."

"Did your father have any enemies, Mr. Mason?"

Ryker Mason looked at him in disbelief. "Sayer Mason, enemies? He had so many I couldn't even list them," said Ryker. "He didn't get to where he was without making enemies—in business, in politics, in his personal…" he stopped.

"In his personal life? Is that what you were going to say Mr. Mason?" asked the District Attorney.

Ryker recovered. "No, of course not," he said, sharply. "In business and in politics. Maybe you should talk to all those protesters outside and up there," he flicked his hand derisively at the public gallery, "the ones who would rather save trees than jobs."

There was an angry reaction to this statement from the public gallery and people leapt to their feet with shouts of "Forest killers!"

Several police officers stationed around the courtroom started to move but the District Attorney raised his voice above the crowd and said, "Order!" in a tone that brooked no opposition. "Sit down and be quiet or these officers will escort you out!"

There was heated chatter and complaining but everyone sat down and stayed quiet.

Keeley had been watching Ryker during the disturbance. Strangely, he was looking not at the protesters in the public gallery but at someone in his family group.

D.A. Bell continued. "Mr. Mason, I know this is difficult for you and your family so let's just proceed as quickly as possible. Who stands to gain by your father's death?"

"Well, our parents were divorced, so everything comes to me and Jack," Ryker continued. "The business was already coming our way, as I said, so that Father could be ready for elected office."

"Is there anything else you can tell us, Mr. Mason? Anything at all that could help us bring your father's murderer to justice?"

Ryker Mason hesitated and Keeley thought she saw him glance at his family again, almost imperceptibly, just as Hewitt Carradine had done.

"No," he said at last, "nothing."

The District Attorney spoke. "I suggest that we hear from two other key witnesses before I invite questions from the jury panel and Counsels. We'll call Mr. Ryker Mason back if necessary. But first let's hear from Mr. Jack Mason and then Mr. Charles Deeds."

Keeley could hear Charles's sharp intake of breath and saw Reid lean towards him, murmuring something. Charles nodded, sat up and looked straight ahead.

Keeley leaned forward and whispered to Charles. *"Are you OK?"*

"The younger brother," Charles whispered back. *"The name Jack Mason..."* he shuddered. *"... he must be named for his great-grandfather, I suppose."* Charles turned away, looking grim.

The District Attorney spoke.

"I call Jack Mason."

Keeley looked curiously at the Mason family group as the security team shuffled aside in their seats and a man stood up. He was wearing dark glasses and kept his head down as he walked towards the witness stand. He looked very different from his brother, his long, light brown hair pulled back behind the collar of his casual sweater, his shirt partly tucked into his jeans.

"Mr. Mason, please state your name."

"Jack Mason," he said, his voice low and sullen.

"Mr. Mason," said the District Attorney, "please take off your dark glasses."

Reluctantly, head down, Jack Mason took off his dark glasses and put them on the shelf in front of him. He raised his head and looked at his brother Ryker, then he turned to face the courtroom.

Without warning, Charles suddenly shot to his feet.

Keeley and Loki looked up at him, shocked, worried that he'd snapped at last.

Charles was pointing at Jack. "I remember!" said Charles, raising his voice. "I remember everything. It was you!"

CHAPTER
TWENTY-SEVEN

Chaos.

Reid was on his feet beside Charles, urging him to sit down. Ryker Mason was shouting at Jack. Hewitt Carradine moved quickly to Jack's side and started speaking to him. Detective Santos stood up and went to stand beside the witness box. The District Attorney was banging his gavel and in the public gallery everyone was on their feet shouting, trying to get a better look at what was happening below.

"Enough! Order!" the District Attorney shouted. "Up there in the public gallery, sit down and be quiet or I'll empty this courtroom. Mr. Summers, control your client." He turned towards Hewitt Carradine. "Approach, please, both Counsels approach." He turned to Jack, who was trying to leave the stand. "Mr. Mason, stay where you are please."

Charles was talking urgently to Reid Summers, spilling out all he remembered, but the District Attorney was repeatedly calling Reid to the bench. Keeley heard Reid tell Charles to stop talking, to wait. Then Reid stood up and spoke to the District Attorney.

"May I request a thirty minute recess, Your Honour? Until this moment my client has had no memory of the events of the night Sayer Mason was killed and it seems that now it has all come back to him. It's urgent to capture his recollections in case they fade again. I want to interview him immediately and request a court stenographer too, so his comments can be read into the record."

Carradine was protesting loudly but since this was an inquest the District Attorney had much more leeway to make decisions than a judge in a typical trial. "Thirty minutes and that's all, Counselor," he said to Reid. "You can use the small room through the door behind my bench. The court stenographer will join you there."

Torrin Bell turned to Jack Mason, who was looking desperately at his brother and his security team. "Mr. Mason, stand down for now, please. Detective Santos, please make sure that none of the witnesses leave." He looked at her and understanding passed between them. She nodded and took up a post at the side door near the Masons.

Reid signalled to Charles and they went to the back room.

Keeley and Loki looked at each other, amazed and fearful.

"I didn't think this day could get any more tense, but it has," Loki said. "Let's try to find a cup of coffee somewhere."

Keeley took his hand and they found a coffee machine just outside the courtroom. The Press and the people from the public gallery were buzzing. Keeley and Loki could hear snatches of conversation, speculation, rumours and gossip.

They took their coffee outside to the back of the courthouse away from the crowd, but this time, instead of sitting in the sun, they paced restlessly.

"What do you think Charles meant when he said, 'It was you'?" Keeley asked Loki.

"I don't know," said Loki, "but it looked like it suddenly all came back to him, all the things he'd forgotten. He recognized Jack Mason but I don't whether that's good or bad, whether it's going to help Charles or hurt him." He paced around the small grass patch and stopped by Keeley.

She looked up at him, grateful for his reassuring presence. "What if Charles knows something dangerous? What if he's in real trouble?" she said, tears coming to her eyes.

"We'll just have to deal with whatever it is. If the truth comes out, that's the best thing that could happen." said Loki.

"Of course, you're right," she said. "This whole thing has been so crazy, right from the moment we found Carter's book."

"Well maybe now we'll all get some answers, at last," said Loki. "I hope so for Charles's sake."

They headed back into the courtroom. Reid and Charles weren't back yet but Carradine, the Mason brothers and their security team were bristling near the side door.

The District Attorney came back in and right behind him came Reid, Charles and the court stenographer.

They took their seats in front of Keeley and Loki. Charles turned round and held out a hand to each of them, which they grasped. "I can't tell you yet, but it will be alright," he said. "Don't worry about me. Everything's going to come out now—everything I've remembered, at least. We'll see where it goes."

The District Attorney called for order.

"There's going to be a change in the order of witnesses," he said. "Mr. Deeds will speak first followed by Mr. Jack Mason. I've determined that this is the best course for us to take. Mr. Deeds, please take the stand."

Charles stood up and walked to the witness box. A ripple of interest rolled through the public gallery and the District Attorney looked up at them and shook his head in warning.

"Please state your name," he said.

"I'm Charles Edward Deeds," he said, with emphasis on the Edward. Keeley and Loki knew why.

"Mr. Deeds, by some remarkable coincidence you've remembered, at the most auspicious moment, what you could not recall until now," said the District Attorney. "Please tell us what that is."

Charles looked him straight in the eye.

"Your Honour," he said, "I'd like everyone to know that I've just told all this to my Counsel in the presence of a court stenographer, to get it all down while I still remembered it. I'm happy to tell it again here, under oath," he said, with strength and authority.

Keeley and Loki nodded encouragingly at him.

The D.A. continued. "Mr. Deeds, please tell us your recollections of the night Sayer Mason was shot. We know you went to the mansion."

Charles spoke. "I flew in from Vancouver the night before and took a taxi from the airport to downtown but I didn't book into a hotel. I rented a car from a small place next to a garage, drove out of the city into a forested area and just parked overnight, trying to figure out what to do. The next day I walked in the forest, drove to a shop nearby, picked up some food, and went back to my parking place in the woods. I needed to confront Mason, Sayer Mason, about his role in the hurt caused to my family in the past but I couldn't face him. It was late by the time I finally got up the courage. I went to the mansion sometime after 8:00 in the evening. Sunday evening."

Keeley looked at the Mason brothers. Jack was no longer hiding behind his security guards but watching Charles warily. He seemed surprised by what Charles had said, but Keeley noticed that Ryker was not. He was watching Charles intently.

Charles went on. "I parked in a corner of Mason's front drive. It's a huge area, a big circular drive and I parked a good distance away from the front door. It was dark by then but I finally got up my courage and went to the door. The housekeeper answered and went to get Mason who came back to the door with her and told her to leave."

"Did you see her leave?" asked Counsel.

"No, by that time I was in Mason's study. I told him that I'd found an old letter accusing his family of doing all kinds of harm to mine many years ago and profiting from it. I told him that his empire was founded on crime, lies and deceit and demanded to know if he was the one who'd sent people to attack my friends and me, to get the letter back."

Carradine was on his feet but the District Attorney silenced him. "I'm assured by Reid Summers, Counsel for Mr. Deeds, and by the police that there is evidence about the authenticity of the letter."

"What?" said Jack Mason, on his feet. "What's going on? What letter?"

"Sit down and shut up, Jack," said Ryker, making no effort to speak softly.

Loki looked at Keeley. "I don't understand. Jack doesn't know about the letter," he said. "But Ryker's not surprised. He knows about it."

Keeley shook her head, baffled. She looked at Charles who had obviously come to the same conclusion and was looking daggers at Ryker Mason.

"Please continue, Mr. Deeds," said the District Attorney, "there'll be time to present the evidence later, just give us the narrative."

"Mason knew what I was talking about," said Charles. "He knew about the letter. He told me I had no proof so I showed him a copy of the letter on my phone. He shouted at me, threatened me, told me to go and get the original or he would hurt my friends, maybe do worse than just hurt them."

Keeley gasped and Loki took her hand.

"He'd sent someone to hurt my friends before," said Charles, "so I knew he meant it."

Carradine was on his feet again and the District Attorney spoke. "There is no evidence that Sayer Mason ordered any attack," he said to the jury. "Mr. Deeds cannot know this for certain."

Charles looked defiant but acknowledged the District Attorney's words and continued. "I was afraid for my friends. I told him I would get the original. I left and went back to my car and just sat there, trying to decide what to do. I'd left the original letter in Vancouver but I hadn't told Mason that. He probably expected me to bring the original right back to him. I think I'd been sitting there for about half an hour, maybe more, when I saw that man, Jack Mason, arrive in a hurry." Charles pointed at Jack, who shook his head in vigorous denial. Charles continued. "I don't think he saw me in my car. He didn't look in my direction and, as I said, I was parked in a dark corner of the driveway.

"He stopped his car right by the front door, rushed up the steps and let himself in. I stayed in my car, paralyzed by fear for my friends and my anger at Mason. I re-read the letter on my phone. I thought about going back in to tell Mason I didn't have the original with me but that I would get it and beg him not to hurt my friends. But I was afraid of the man who'd arrived, the man I now know to be Jack Mason."

"No!" said Jack Mason, on his feet again.

"Be quiet, Mr. Mason," said the District Attorney. "You'll have your turn to tell your side of the story. Sit down and be quiet. Please continue Mr. Deeds."

"I thought perhaps Sayer Mason had called in another of his thugs," said Charles. "I was afraid. They attacked my friend at the shop in Cascade Canyon. And they sent people to shoot at a friend and myself in the forest in North Vancouver. I know what the Masons are capable of. Look what they did to my family."

"Mr. Deeds," the District Attorney cautioned, "stick to the facts as you recall them."

Charles shook his head in frustration and continued. "I decided to call Mr. Summers to get advice but I wanted to get somewhere safe first. So I started my car and drove around the circular drive on my way out. As I passed the front door he…," he pointed at Jack Mason again, "Jack Mason, came storming out. I was really afraid then and drove away as fast as I could. I managed to get down the road and into the woodland part of the neighbourhood but then I saw a car coming up fast behind me. I knew it was him, who else could it be?"

"Mr. Deeds…" the District Attorney warned. But Charles went on, determined to tell his story at last.

"The car came up behind me and smashed into me. I lost control and went off the road into the ditch. I hit my head on the steering wheel but I was still conscious when he dragged me out of the car and hit me several times. It was him, Jack Mason. I'm sure of it. That's all I remember until I woke up in hospital."

The public gallery erupted in chaos again and Counsels were clamouring to be heard.

Keeley looked at the Masons. Ryker had grabbed his brother by the arm and was talking to him heatedly. One of the men on the security team was leaning close, trying to intervene.

Again the District Attorney raised his voice, instructing the police and court officials. "Clear the public gallery! Everyone else, please stay where you are," he said. There were shouts of protest but police moved quickly and within minutes order was restored. Ryker and Jack Mason took their seats again, separated and restrained by several members of their security team. Ryker was still trying to reach his brother, angrily struggling to shake off the man who held him.

"Mr. Carradine," said the District Attorney, "please control your clients and come forward if you wish to question this witness."

Hewitt Carradine stood up and spoke sharply to Ryker, who fell silent and sat still. Then he walked slowly towards the witness box.

"Mr. Deeds," he said in a calm, authoritative voice, "I know this must be very difficult for you. You've experienced an injury and severe stress. I'll try to make my questions as straightforward as possible."

Charles looked at him suspiciously, guessing the direction of his questions.

Carradine continued. "Mr. Deeds, is it possible that all of this, this sudden recovery of memories, could be nothing more than your imagination filling in painful blanks? Could you not have simply made up all of this?"

"No," said Charles. "I did not make it up. I am absolutely sure that Jack Mason is the one who hit my car and attacked me. And…" he looked at Reid, who nodded his agreement, knowing what was to come, "if you take a look at Jack Mason's car there will be proof. He can't have hit me without doing damage to his own vehicle. Even if he got it fixed, there will be a record."

Carradine pursued his point. "Isn't it true, Mr. Deeds, that you had considerable cause to hate Sayer Mason and do him harm? Why should the police not turn their attention back to you?"

Charles stayed quiet, looking at the Masons, then at Keeley, Loki and Reid. Then he spoke, his voice strong and convincing. "I had cause to hate him but I would never have done him harm. I welcome any police involvement, Mr. Carradine. I have nothing to hide. I want the most thorough investigation and I will cooperate fully as long as that investigation includes Jack Mason. After all, and I can't prove this yet as you know, unless there is some random killer out there it looks as if Jack Mason was the last person to see his father alive."

Carradine fixed Charles with a forceful gaze. "That's not for you to say, Mr. Deeds," he said. "Only Jack Mason can answer that."

Keeley turned to Loki. *"Why isn't Carradine pushing harder?"* she whispered. *"What's going on?"*

"I don't know," Loki whispered back, *"I thought he would throw everything at Charles and try to break his story."*

"Mr. Carradine, have you finished questioning Mr. Deeds?" asked the District Attorney.

"For now, Your Honour, yes," said Carradine. Ryker Mason muttered something but Carradine ignored it.

"Then we will hear from Jack Mason again," said the District Attorney.

"Your Honour, may I request some time to talk with my clients?" asked Carradine. "Mr. Deeds's testimony raised many questions. I'll need time to talk with Jack and Ryker Mason about all this."

The District Attorney looked at his watch. "That's reasonable, Mr. Carradine. In fact, let's adjourn for the day. We'll reconvene tomorrow morning at nine sharp. Mr. Deeds, you may step down. Detective Santos, may I have a word with you after we adjourn please?"

Charles rejoined Keeley, Loki and Reid. Reid suggested that they all go to his office, order some food and debrief. As they were leaving Keeley looked back to see Detective Santos in deep conversation with the District Attorney. As Santos walked away from the District Attorney's bench she caught Keeley looking back at her and nodded once, quickly, as if to say she could see the light at the end of the tunnel.

CHAPTER
TWENTY-EIGHT

They sat around on comfortable chairs in Reid Summers's bright office. Reid sat at his desk and ordered Chinese food from his favourite place and they all began to relax.

"How do you feel, Charles?" asked Loki. "It must be a relief to remember at last."

"It is, it really is a relief," said Charles. "I wondered if I would ever get my memory back. But it's complicated now, isn't it? The Masons will close ranks and we know they can be formidable enemies. Their best strategy now would be to discredit me, make everyone doubt my testimony. I'm still afraid for all of us. Sayer Mason stopped at nothing to get what he wanted. No one got in his way. And I believe that Jack Mason is just like his father." He turned to Reid. "Should I be concerned for the safety of my friends?"

Reid left his desk and came to sit with them.

"Charles, I need to let you know about a couple of things," he said. Charles tensed but Reid was quick to reassure him. "No, no, it's OK. Don't worry. As we discussed I asked the District Attorney to talk with Detective Santos about taking a look at Jack Mason's vehicle. There should still be some evidence of him forcing you off the road, damage, or maybe even something from a repair shop, And there's something else he might not have thought about. Some vehicles have a kind of 'black box', a passive GPS tracking device. If Jack Mason's vehicle has one it might still have a record of his movements that night."

They all looked at Reid in amazement.

"Passive GPS tracking?" asked Keeley. "I didn't even know such a thing existed."

"Not all vehicles have them," said Reid. "But if you use a navigation device with maps to help you get from one place to another, there's a chance it's capturing your travelling history."

"We'd have him then, wouldn't we?" said Charles softly. "Is it admissible?"

"Yes, in an inquest," said Reid. "The rules are not as strict as in a trial. I believe Detective Santos will try to get it admitted if it exists. If she finds that Mason had his car repaired after that night, she can certainly enter that."

They all sat in silence, lost in their own thoughts. Then a knock on the door announced the Chinese food and their spirits lifted. They laughed and chatted together until Charles said, "I'm so tired, dear friends. I think I'll head back to the hotel and have a quiet evening."

"We'll go with you Charles," said Keeley. "I could use some quiet time myself."

"I'll call you if I hear anything at all," said Reid to Charles. "Try not to worry, if that's possible. I think we have the upper hand here. I'll pick you up at eight o'clock tomorrow at the hotel, Charles. That will give us time to go over things before proceedings start again."

They went their separate ways. Keeley and Loki decided to have a glass of wine in the bar but Charles said he just wanted to rest. Keeley hugged him. "See you at the courthouse tomorrow Charles. But if there's anything you need before that, anything at all, please come and find us."

Charles smiled at them both and walked away slowly, his head bowed in thought.

"What a day!" said Loki. "Unbelievable! The good thing is that Charles has his memory back. Apart from everything else it means that he's fully recovered from his head injury."

Keeley nodded in agreement. "I'm going to call Arwen and Elizabeth when we get back to the room and let them know what's happened. Will you call Rory and Declan?"

"I will. They'll be so relieved," said Loki, reaching for her hand.

She took it, reassured by his optimism. "One surprise after another," she said. "What will tomorrow bring, I wonder?"

When they got to the courtroom in the morning they found that things had changed. There were guards on the doors. The Press and the public were not going to be allowed in. Keeley and Loki were held back with the rest of the crowd but Loki texted Charles who was already inside. Charles came to the door and talked to the guard, who reluctantly let them in.

The courtroom was virtually empty. Ryker Mason was there, looking grim and exhausted. The Mason security people were beside him. Jack Mason was nowhere to be seen.

Police were at every door. The court stenographer was at her desk. The jury panel were in their seats, talking quietly to each other.

Hewitt Carradine, Detective Santos and Reid were huddled in front of the District Attorney's bench. The District Attorney himself was listening to their conversation, making occasional remarks. Carradine was arguing quietly but vigorously with Detective Santos, who clearly remained unmoved. Reid was watchful, interjecting frequently.

Charles took his seat in the front row. Keeley and Loki sat behind him, in their usual seats.

"*What's going on, Charles?*" whispered Loki.

"*I don't know,*" said Charles quietly. "*When we got here the District Attorney closed the court and called Counsels to the front.*"

They all sat without speaking, eyes on the group at the front.

At nine sharp the District Attorney asked everyone to return to their seats.

"Members of the jury panel, thank you for your patience. There are some new developments that have changed the direction of this inquest. I call Detective Santos to the stand."

Detective Santos walked briskly to the stand and stated her name.

"Detective Santos," said D.A. Bell, "on my instruction you've investigated Jack Mason's vehicle. Can you tell us what you found?"

"Yes sir," she said. "His vehicle still shows slight damage to the front grille and there are paint scrapes that we believe will match the vehicle driven by Mr. Deeds on the night of Sayer Mason's murder. We're waiting for those test results."

"Is there anything else, Detective Santos?" he asked.

"Yes, we located a passive GPS tracker in Jack Mason's navigation program. It shows that on the night in question the vehicle was driven to the Mason mansion and arrived there at 9:16 p.m., stayed there until 9:25 p.m. then left. It also shows that at 9:30 p.m. Jack Mason's vehicle stopped at the same location where Mr. Deeds was run off the road."

Charles glanced back at Keeley and Loki.

"Is there any evidence to show that it was Jack Mason driving the vehicle?" asked the District Attorney.

"Not yet. We're looking at CCTV footage in the Hillside neighbourhood again," said Detective Santos. "And I've ordered a full forensic examination of the vehicle."

"Thank you Detective Santos, please step down," the District Attorney said. He turned to Hewitt Carradine. "Where is Jack Mason, Mr. Carradine?"

Carradine leaned over and spoke to Ryker Mason, whose face was a mask of pain and anger. Ryker said nothing but nodded vehemently.

"May I approach, please?" asked Carradine.

"Take the stand Mr. Carradine," said the District Attorney. "You're still under oath and it will be easier for everyone to hear what you say."

Hewitt Carradine stepped into the witness box. He looked at Charles, then at Ryker and began to speak.

"Your Honour," he said, "and members of the jury, Jack Mason's whereabouts are unknown. It seems he has left Portland. He must have had help to do this as I know Detective Santos was keeping him under surveillance. I'm here to speak now for Ryker Mason, who has instructed me to disclose information important to this case."

Charles sat up in his seat and Keeley leaned forward to put a hand on his shoulder.

"Sayer Mason was not going to hand over half of his business to Jack," said Hewitt Carradine. "He was going to disinherit him."

There were several gasps of surprise in the room and the District Attorney held up his hand for silence. "Please go on, Mr. Carradine."

"It came to my attention," said Carradine, "while putting together all the necessary paperwork for the business transition, that something was amiss with Jack Mason. His brother was worried about him and asked me to investigate. Jack was running with a dangerous crowd, some of them serious criminals. He was spending money on drugs and alcohol, not showing up for work, getting into debt."

The District Attorney spoke. "You have evidence of all of this, Mr. Carradine?"

"Yes," said Carradine, "this and more. I looked deeper into Jack Mason's life and discovered that his birth was the result of an affair between Sayer Mason's ex-wife and a known gang member. He was not Sayer Mason's son. And Jack knew it. He'd always known it. His mother had told him, but he—and she—wanted his inheritance and would do anything to get it. Once Jack took over the business as an equal partner with Ryker he would have been able to get his hands on enormous wealth."

He looked at Ryker, who seemed to brace himself for what was coming next.

"When I told Sayer about this, about two weeks before he died, he was stunned and angry," said Carradine. "He asked me to bring him proof that Jack was not his son and he told me that if he found it convincing he would confront Jack and tell him he was going to disinherit him, cut him out of his life completely. I took the files to Sayer but I did not tell Ryker what I'd found. I wanted to leave that to Sayer. I knew Sayer was going to confront Jack but I didn't know when, until Mr. Deeds testified. Sayer must have ordered Jack to go and see him that night. I suspect he told Jack over the phone what it was about. Sayer was never one to mince words. That would explain why Jack arrived in a rage."

He looked again at Ryker, who had his head in his hands. "Ryker knew nothing of this until after Sayer was murdered. We had no reason to believe that Sayer had ever spoken with Jack about it. Jack gave the police an alibi for his whereabouts, that I now suspect was bought and paid for. The murder consumed us all after that, the business was in chaos and instead of an orderly transition it became a battle for all the pieces of the empire. Sayer had many enemies. We thought it would only be a matter of time until one of them was caught and accused of his murder."

He turned to Charles and spoke directly to him. "Mr. Deeds," he said, "Ryker and I are appalled by what you've been through. Jack knew nothing about the letter that brought you here, so that couldn't have been a factor for him. He came after you because he knew you'd seen him at the mansion."

He paused, taking time to think about what to say next. "But Sayer always knew about the letter. He told me when I first became his lawyer decades ago that he'd been looking for it for years—that he had people who would get it back for him if it ever surfaced. I didn't know about the contents, just that it was part of his family history. If I'd known, I might have pre-empted the attack on the individual in Cascade Canyon."

He looked at Keeley, Loki and Charles. "I'm so deeply sorry. Sayer didn't tell me that the letter had resurfaced. He had a letter too, of which I was unaware, written by your grandfather Joseph, Mr. Deeds, to Sayer's grandfather Jack. It's how he knew what was in your letter and where it was hidden. Sayer's letter was sealed and kept in his safe, to be opened after his death. Ryker opened it after his father was killed and showed it to me."

Charles slumped forward and put his head in his hands. Across the room, Ryker Mason raised his head and looked at Charles. Keeley thought she could see sympathy and compassion there, the understanding of a terrible family history shared.

CHAPTER
TWENTY-NINE

Carradine was still speaking to Charles but Charles could not look at him. "Mr. Deeds," he said, "Ryker Mason has asked me to say that if you'd be willing, he'd like to meet with you to talk about all this."

Charles looked up then, fear and suspicion in his eyes. There was too much water under the bridge. He shook his head.

Carradine understood. "Time enough for that," he said, turning to the District Attorney. "Back to the business at hand. What is your advice, Your Honour?"

The District Attorney answered. "Detective Santos has told me the police are looking for Jack Mason. He's now the chief suspect in the murder of Sayer Mason. A thorough investigation will take place." He looked at Ryker. "Mr. Mason, thank you for instructing Mr. Carradine to reveal this information. You've put aside what must be deep personal distress and grief to make sure the truth comes to light. I see no reason to think you had any involvement in this."

Charles raised his head then and spoke angrily. "Are you sure, sir, are you sure? Why should we believe him? How could anyone ever trust a Mason?"

"Mr. Deeds, I'll forgive your outburst under the circumstances but please don't let it happen again," said the District Attorney. "Mr. Carradine is a respected attorney here in Portland. If he says he has evidence to support his testimony, he'll produce it. If he says that Ryker Mason knew nothing about the letter, you can believe him. I think we know now that the letter had nothing to do with you being attacked. It seems likely that was an attempt to silence a material witness to Sayer Mason's murder. I know you have questions about the attacks that took place in British Columbia but those are not at issue here. That must be pursued separately."

Charles shook his head in frustration and disbelief.

The District Attorney continued, "Members of the jury panel, please don't talk about what has taken place here today. You're still under oath and will be required to return at a future date. For now, I'm going to adjourn this inquest until Jack Mason is found." He stood up, walked to the back of the room and disappeared through the door.

The court clerk instructed the jury panel to leave by the side door.

Charles, Reid, Keeley and Loki stayed in their seats, trying to absorb what had just happened and unwilling to face the clamouring Press and public outside the courtroom doors.

Charles was speaking to Reid when he became aware that someone had come to stand beside him. He looked up to see Ryker Mason. Charles recoiled in fear and surprise but Ryker stood his ground.

"Mr. Deeds," Ryker said, his voice so soft and broken that Charles instinctively leaned forward to catch his words. "Mr. Deeds, I don't know what to say but I know I have to say something to you after all the years of pain and hurt…" he stopped and tried again. "…after all the years of my family hurting yours. Nothing I say can change that now. I'm the last Mason left who can make amends." Tears came to his bright, clear eyes and he angrily shook them away. "I'm the last person left who can say I'm sorry. Not enough, I know, not nearly enough…" he turned and walked away. Charles got up quickly and went after him.

Reid, Loki and Keeley went on high alert and stood up, ready for anything. Charles reached Ryker and put his hand on his shoulder. Ryker spun around, surprised, wary. But Charles simply dropped his hand and said, "Mr. Mason, I'm the last too, the last one in my family who can put this all to rest once and for all. Let's meet and talk about it. We have a hundred years of history to put right." He held out his hand and Ryker grasped it and shook it firmly.

"Let's not wait," said Ryker. "Can we meet tomorrow?" He looked over at Keeley and Loki. "And please bring your friends and Mr. Summers if you want to."

"Tomorrow is fine," said Charles. "And I think it should just be the two of us."

Reid, who'd been hovering nearby, offered to be the go-between to arrange the meeting. Keeley and Loki had watched all this in astonishment. When Charles held his hand out and Ryker took it Keeley burst into tears. The weight of history had fallen heavily on all of them. After a hundred years two good men had faced down corruption, tragedy, death and deceit and reached towards each other for redemption.

Loki took Keeley's hand. "Look," he said, and pointed to the wall behind the witness box. In an alcove stood a small statue of Justice, blindfolded, scales in her hand. Anubis, thought Keeley. Even here, even after 3,000 years, he makes his presence felt.

Reid took them out the back way and they avoided the crowds, although one reporter spotted them and began to chase them down. Reid and Loki dispatched him in no uncertain terms and they made their way to Reid's car.

"I'm not sure where we should go now," said Reid, his hand on the key in the ignition. "It's a celebration, a victory for you Charles, but somehow it doesn't seem right to go and drink champagne."

They all agreed. "But we should do something," said Charles. "For me, it feels as if the earth has shifted on its axis. I have a great sense of peace, a huge weight lifted, one I've carried for many years. I don't want to forget this moment. I want to mark it, somehow."

"I have an idea," said Reid. "It's still early in the day and the sun is shining, which, as we all know, is a gift here in the Pacific Northwest. There's a beautiful Japanese Garden here in Portland. Let's go there and walk those peaceful paths. We can have tea and let nature do her work."

It was the perfect place to go.

As they walked together through the imposing Nezu Gate and into the gardens, a great sense of calm descended on them all. They didn't speak, each lost in their own thoughts. Reid led them down the path and they strolled around a pond bordered by rocks, plants and trees chosen for their harmony and beauty. They walked slowly across a moon bridge, reaching the elegant pagoda lantern on the other side and stopping to drink in the deep, healing serenity of nature.

Smiling at each other, breathing deeply, they wandered through the many different gardens, across stepping stones and past Heavenly Falls with its terraces of falling water sparkling in the early afternoon light. They stood beside the flawlessly raked sand in the stone garden, its lines and circles and perfectly placed stones calling them to contemplate the beauty of empty space. With every step they could feel the anxiety and pain of the past few months dropping away.

Reid spoke first, quietly, lifting them out of their reverie. "Look," he said, pointing through the vine maples, shore pines and Douglas firs, and into the distance. "Mt. Hood."

And there it was—a perfect, snow-capped volcanic cone, mirroring its Japanese counterparts around the Pacific Ring of Fire. They were in awe.

Charles came to stand between Keeley and Loki, linking arms with each of them. "I know now that everything will be alright," he said. "This garden reminds us that a hundred years is nothing to rocks, trees and mountains. Ryker and I will find a way to make peace."

"On that note," said Reid. "let's go and have tea." He led the way back through the Nezu gate to the Umami Café, a tranquil, simple structure of wood and glass suspended over the hillside. Reid ordered classic Japanese tea served Tokyo style, with a selection of mouth-watering local cakes. He insisted on pouring for them. "We won't talk shop here," he said, echoing what they were all thinking. "We'll go back to my office after this and figure out what comes next. But for now, we'll just enjoy this lovely place."

Sharing the ritual of taking tea together, which resonated across so many cultures, they all appreciated the tangible bonds of friendship and trust between them. Over tea, time seemed to relax its grip on them and let them refresh, recover and renew.

They left the gardens feeling completely different from when they'd arrived. Balance had returned and fear had retreated. Keeley and Loki asked Reid to drop them at the hotel. Reid and Charles had a lot to discuss.

"I'll come and find you later," said Charles. "Perhaps we can have dinner together."

"Just knock on our door when you get back, Charles," said Loki.

Back at the hotel Keeley turned to Loki. "I feel as if I've just had a meditation session or a yoga class," she said. "It's crazy to feel like this after what happened in court today, but I do. I think I'll just lie down for a while and try to sleep before dinner. I was so anxious last night that I hardly slept at all."

"I like that idea," said Loki. "Will it disturb you if I come in and read while you sleep?"

She smiled at him and put her arms around him. "I'd love that," she said quietly. "Let's go up to our room."

Anyone watching them would simply have seen two people lost in each other's company, obviously in love, without a care in the world.

CHAPTER THIRTY

When Charles knocked on their door in the early evening they were up, dressed, rested and ready for dinner.

"Hello, you two," he said, cheerfully. "Lots to tell you. All good. Can you recommend a pub? Somewhere we can get some hearty food, nurse a beer or two and talk?"

They were happy to see him in such high spirits.

"Well, my good sir," said Loki, "As a purveyor of fine books, I feel I must recommend the Pen & Tablet. Good food, good beer, good whisky and enough enthusiastic good cheer around us that we won't be overheard. And not far away."

They all laughed. How things had changed since the morning, thought Keeley. She'd wanted to phone everyone at home and tell them about it but after talking it over with Loki they'd both decided to wait, given the District Attorney's advice to keep the courtroom proceedings confidential. Reid had told them that the District Attorney would hold a press conference in two days. Until then, all information was sealed. They would be back in Cascade Canyon by then and would be able to tell everyone in person before they heard it on the news.

They sat at a table in the corner of the Pen & Tablet, beers in hand, orders placed. Loki was right, there was enough animated conversation and happy chatter around them that they would not be overheard if they were careful.

Loki launched into it. "What can you tell us, Charles?"

"Well," said Charles, "I'll tell you everything I know, everything Reid and I talked about. They haven't caught up with Jack Mason—if we're still calling him that—yet. Reid thinks they'll get him soon because he's been so careless. And Reid thinks there's enough evidence to charge him with Sayer's murder, with more evidence coming to light now they know where to look."

"Great news!" said Loki.

"It is," said Charles. "And Ryker phoned Reid while I was there. Reid thought it would be best to meet at his office and I feel comfortable with that. It feels safe. So Ryker and I will meet there at ten o'clock tomorrow morning."

"Wow," said Keeley, reaching for Charles's hand. "That's a huge step, Charles. Will you be okay?"

Charles took her hand and held it for a moment, looking at her kind face. "I welcome it now," he said. "It's the right thing to do. Life has given Ryker and me the chance for redemption and we're going to take it. And after that I think we should all go home to Cascade Canyon." He beamed at them. "I have a cabin to move into!"

By noon the following day they were heading home to Canada. Charles had come back from his meeting with Ryker in a pensive mood. Keeley and Loki hadn't wanted to bombard him with questions so they all got their bags packed, caught a taxi to the airport and boarded the plane.

They sat in a row of three, Charles by the window, Loki next to him and Keeley on the aisle. Once they were in the air with cups of tea in hand, Charles leaned towards them and said, in a quiet voice, "It seems like I'm always saying this, but I owe you both so much. You've given me my life back, saved me from the curses of the past. And then, for you to stand beside me through all of this…I'll never be able to thank you enough."

"Don't sell yourself short Charles," said Keeley, smiling at him. "We love being your friends. You came into our lives and made us part of your amazing story. Rory and Declan and the students feel the same way. The whole village is pleased you've chosen to stay, not the least Maren Quayle!"

Charles laughed. "It's true, isn't it? We've all been on this journey together since finding the book and the letter." He suddenly became serious. "Speaking of letters, let me tell you about the one Ryker showed me, the one my grandfather Joseph wrote to Ryker's great-grandfather, Jack. Ryker found it when he was going through Sayer's papers. I have a copy."

He pulled a piece of paper from his pocket and handed it to Loki. Keeley leaned in to read it with him. They recognized Joseph's writing.

Mason, I know you will come looking for her. She is gone. You know what she has done, what you both have done. She took everything from me, my life, my profession, my possessions. She told me all this tonight. I could have forgiven her all of that, perhaps, but she did something else. She nearly killed my little son. On purpose, for evil curiosity. She blinded him. Because of her they took him away from me forever. I can never forgive that, never forget. She laughed as she told me how she'd hurt Teddy. She said she'd hoped he would die, because then she would have found a new poison, an ancient poison. She taunted me and mocked Teddy and I picked up a stone ushabti from Thebes and hit her with it. Strange that it begins and ends with Egypt. She fell and did not get up. I killed her and now she's killed me. But the future will have its revenge, Mason. I've written the whole story in a letter to my son Teddy, about all the evil things you both did, how she tried to murder him, the theft, the lies, the deliberate pain you inflicted. One day, when you least expect it, it will all come back to haunt you. Wherever you run, you can never hide from the evil you did here. It will stalk you down the years. I've hidden the letter where you can never find it, in Carter's book, the one I bought when all of this began, when she tricked us in New York and wormed her way into our family. Don't bother looking for it. It's not here. You can tear the place apart but you won't find it. But what do I care now? I'm going to let the Black River take me into oblivion. I buried her in unconsecrated ground, contaminated now by her bones. Her heart will crash to earth when they weigh it on the Scales of Anubis against the feather of Maat. A curse be on you and all who come after you. And as for me, I throw myself on the mercy of Anubis. Perhaps there is a quiet place in the Field of Rushes where my soul will find peace at last.

Keeley and Loki finished reading and looked at Charles, who was watching them anxiously, willing them to understand. It was a lot to comprehend, a lot to accept.

When Loki spoke, his feelings were evident. "It's over now, my friend. Over for them, over for you. It's all come to light. You can put it behind you. You and Ryker."

Charles nodded, relieved by their reaction.

"Charles, did you always know your grandfather had taken his own life?" asked Keeley, gently. There was no point in turning away from the hard questions now.

Charles appreciated the directness. It helped him stay in control. "I knew he'd drowned in the Black River," he said. "But my father thought it was an accident. That was the official verdict. There was obviously someone left in Watertown who cared enough about my father to protect his reputation, even in the face of all that had happened.

"There's something else," he went on. "Ryker is as sure as he can be that his father ordered the attempted theft of Carter's book, when Declan was attacked. And that his brother sent the men who came after us when we were hiking, Loki, to stop me from identifying him. Ryker's going to give the police all the hiring records of the security group Sayer and Jack Mason used."

"What will you do about this, Charles, you and Ryker? Can you put it all behind you?" asked Loki.

"I'm not sure and neither is he," said Charles. "At the moment he has no wish to go to Watertown and dig up the past. Neither do I. But I'll respect whatever he does. He's lost everything as well, through no fault of his own. And he's still a young man, with his life ahead of him."

"Will he still run for office, do you think?" asked Keeley.

"I think so. I think he should. He seems to be an ethical man and he'd be so different from his father. Polar opposite. I think he can do good. I've told him that I'll support any choice he makes, both privately and publicly, so that none of this terrible business damages his reputation. He doesn't deserve that." He looked out of the window at the mountains and the ocean unfolding beneath them.

"The curse ends here and now," he said.

They sat back in their seats, lost in thought. Then a slight downward shift in the altitude of the plane let them know that they had crossed the border into Canada and were descending into Vancouver Airport. Coming home.

As they drove out of the airport Charles's phone rang. It was Reid. Jack Mason had been caught. Hoping to bargain his way to a more lenient sentence, he'd confessed. It was over.

CHAPTER THIRTY-ONE

March came in like a lion. The winds roared down from the high mountains, bringing with them a breath of snow. But the sun shone bright. In the woods and gardens around Cascade Canyon the first signs of spring were making their way through the dark earth to the light.

In Keeley's garden the daffodils and snowdrops made their enchanting entrance. Keeley gathered them, perfect messengers of better days to come. She walked down the street in the mid-day sunshine, past Bean Cabin where Peter and Yvonne, laden with baskets and boxes, were making their way down the steps. Loki was with them and he joined Keeley, catching her hand in his. At the end of the street Mr. and Mrs. Ito came out to walk with them and they slowed their pace, strolling easily, talking together, spirits high.

They walked to the far end of the village and up the long driveway. Keeley recognized Maren's car and Scott's truck. The door to Charles's cabin stood open. Happy conversation and laughter echoed from inside and the new arrivals stepped through the door to join in. The students were already there. Arwen was helping Maren in the kitchen, setting out plates of food beneath the rack of gleaming copper pots. Peter and Yvonne went to join them. Keeley watched Peter carefully place a box in the fridge. Cream horns. That simple thought filled her with joy. This was the best of times.

Charles and Sherine were setting out plates and glasses on the old pine table from Past Life. Scott came in through the back door with an armload of wood, which he stacked by the fireplace. He stopped to stoke the fire, turned and smiled at all the new arrivals and walked over to Mr. and Mrs. Ito.

"We've set out our favourite chairs for you by the fire," he said, enthusiastically. "Let me show you." Keeley smiled at 'our favourite chairs'. She knew Scott had chosen the chairs for Charles when they first came in to Past Life and he was very proud of them. Mrs. Ito took Scott's arm and smiled up at him as he escorted her gently to the chair. Mr. Ito went to the fireplace, running his hands over the old stones, feeling their stories.

Charles came over to welcome them all. He looked happy, relaxed and proud. "Come in, come in!" he said. "Welcome to my humble abode."

Keeley and Loki had just stepped inside when there was a knock on the door. Rory and Declan stood there peering through two huge potted plants. "Look who we found!" said Rory. He moved his plant aside and Elizabeth stepped forward.

"I couldn't miss this," she said. "I flew in from LA this morning and Rory and Declan picked me up from the airport."

Charles gave her a long hug. "Welcome, old friend," he said. "I'm so glad you made it. Could you ever have imagined our travels would bring us here together?"

"Never," she said, smiling at him. "Our love of ancient things has taken us to some interesting places, Charles, but your adventure beats all."

Rory and Declan presented Charles with their plants. He asked them to put them on either side of the fireplace. "Give us a tour, then?" said Declan.

"Of course," said Charles, "I'd love to. First, come and see Maren."

They started for the kitchen but were interrupted by voices at the front door. Luc and Tom were there with their families, the children bouncing up and down in their eagerness to get inside.

"Come on in, all of you!" said Charles. He walked towards them and Tasha, Tom's little daughter, broke away from her parents and ran towards him, remembering their happy encounter at the Christmas party. Charles caught her in his arms and lifted her into the air. "Well, it's truly a party now you're here, Miss Tasha," he said. Tasha giggled delightedly as he put her back down. "Go on into the kitchen," he said to her. "I think you'll find that Mrs. Quayle has some special treats for you." She ran off with all the kids following noisily behind her.

It was happy, boisterous and full of energy with so many people in the small cabin. The students, as promised, had organized everything and planned a great feast. Charles had acquired some fine wine and excellent local beer and everyone had brought food to share. For the kids, Arwen and Sherine had organized toys and games and even a treasure hunt in the garden. Magically, every child found a treasure. Several of the adults joined in. Maren, with the help of Elizabeth, was kept busy making hot chocolate for the excited treasure hunters.

It was late in the afternoon when Tom and Elaine and Luc and Sara gathered up their children and said their farewells. As they all trooped out of the front door, Charles took Luc and Tom aside. "This wouldn't be happening without you both of you," he said, seriously. "Luc, thanks for giving me the benefit of the doubt and for staying on the case until it was solved. Tom, without you and Reid I don't know where I'd be now."

Tom put his hand on Charles's shoulder. "Charles, it's my job, but it's more than that. You're a friend now, part of this community." He smiled and looked down the driveway to where Tasha had stopped and was waving frantically to Charles, who saw her and waved back. Satisfied, she did a little leap into the air and ran to catch up with her mother. They all laughed. "You're in," said Tom with a grin. "What more can I say?" He shook Charles's hand and went to join his family.

"I'm glad you ended up on the right side of the law, Charles," said Luc in a stern tone that he couldn't sustain. He smiled, shrugged and clapped Charles on the back before walking down the driveway towards Sara and the kids.

The students were happily taking all the leftovers back to their rooms at the university. After hugs all round they loaded everything into Scott's truck and headed away, waving out of the open windows as they left.

Peter and Yvonne said their goodbyes with an invitation to come in for cream horns the next day. They were going to accompany Mr. and Mrs. Ito on a slow stroll home.

On the front doorstep, Kaito Ito put his hand gently on Charles's arm. "Mr. Deeds…Charles-san," he said in his quiet voice, "I asked Scott to bring this here for you." He held out his hand to a corner of the wild garden. A beautiful lidded pot stood there, glazed in rich green, the colour of the deep forest. Charles recognized it and drew in a deep breath. "It belongs here with you," said Kaito. "Let it stay where it is and age with the forest around it. Things become more beautiful with the passage of time."

Charles, caught up in the wonder of the moment, bowed deeply to Kaito, who bowed back, turned, and taking his wife's hand, went to join Peter and Yvonne at the foot of the driveway.

Rory and Declan, still in high spirits, made the rounds of saying goodbye. At the door, Declan took Charles aside. "You're home now, Charles, where you belong. Take it from someone who's come from far away, we'll always feel a pull to other places. But this place, Cascade Canyon, it has something special. You feel it don't you? The people here are dear, good people. You'll never regret making your home here."

Charles was too emotional to answer, thinking about all that Declan had been through, but he gripped Declan's hand as Rory and Elizabeth came to the door. Elizabeth was staying with Declan and Rory overnight before flying out the next day. She hugged Charles. "Next time you have an adventure, old friend, I want to be in on it, but please don't make it quite as exciting as this one!"

Charles waved goodbye to them all and went back inside. Keeley and Loki were sitting by the fire talking with Maren. Charles, his eyes bright with happiness, sat down next to Maren on the old green leather loveseat from Past Life.

"We have something for you too, Charles," said Loki, "some books to warm your house." Keeley gave Charles the book about ski cabins and Loki gave him the story of the lost Japanese village. Charles, delighted, showed them to Maren. Then Loki said, "There's one more, Charles, from Folios, from both of us."

Loki produced a beautiful book. Maren recognized the cover and nodded. "Perfect," she said.

"It's not as old as another book we're all familiar with," said Loki, "but that was the old world and this is the new." He held out the book to Charles. On the cover, a First Nations artist had painted a raven carrying the sun. "These are the legends of your new home."

"There's a beautiful story in the book," said Keeley, "about Raven bringing the first light to the human world to banish the darkness."

Charles took the book from Loki and looked at the picture on the cover. "Thank you. It's wonderful," he said. "This is just what it feels like to me, coming full circle out of the darkness of the past into the sunlight here in Cascade Canyon."

Keeley and Loki said goodbye, promising to see Charles and Maren at Bean Cabin in the morning. When they reached the end of the driveway they turned and waved. Charles stood there at the door, his arm raised in farewell, Maren at his side, with all the warmth and light of the cabin glowing brightly behind them.

"Home," said Keeley. Loki reached for her hand and they walked away down the forest path.

EPILOGUE

Light came. The ghosts of a hundred years were released at last to face the Scales of Anubis. Some, with hearts hanging heavy in the balance, were cast into outer darkness, their eternal journeys extinguished. But others, whose souls were weighed against truth and justice and found to be lighter than feathers, began the great crossing to the afterlife, free to live and love in eternal sunshine, untroubled by the passage of time.

Milton Keynes UK
Ingram Content Group UK Ltd.
UKHW021804270524
443037UK00001B/37

9 781038 305091